REUNION WITH HIS SURGEON PRINCESS

KARIN BAINE

MILLS & BOON

First published in Great Britain 2020
by Mills & Boon, an imprint of HarperCollins*Publishers*
1 London Bridge Street, London, SE1 9GF

Large Print edition 2020

© 2020 Karin Baine

ISBN: 978-0-263-08602-7

MIX
Paper from
responsible sources
FSC **FSC C007454**
www.fsc.org

This book is produced from independently certified FSC™ paper to ensure responsible forest management. For more information visit www.harpercollins.co.uk/green.

Printed and bound in Great Britain
by CPI Group (UK) Ltd, Croydon, CR0 4YY

Karin Baine lives in Northern Ireland with her husband, two sons and her out-of-control notebook collection. Her mother and her grandmother's vast collection of books inspired her love of reading and her dream of becoming a Mills & Boon author. Now she can tell people she has a *proper* job! You can follow Karin on Twitter, @karinbaine1, or visit her website for the latest news— karinbaine.com.

Also by Karin Baine

The Courage to Love Her Army Doc
Falling for the Foster Mum
Reforming the Playboy
Their Mistletoe Baby
From Fling to Wedding Ring
Midwife Under the Mistletoe
The Single Dad's Proposal
Their One-Night Twin Surprise
Their One-Night Christmas Gift
Healed by Their Unexpected Family

Discover more at millsandboon.co.uk.

For Tammy and Kieran xx

CHAPTER ONE

'I NEED YOU.' Apparently, that was all Kaja had to say after five years apart to get Seth Davenport back in her life.

Now here he was striding through the airport in his short-sleeved, blue cotton shirt and linen trousers, wrinkled from the flight. Time and distance melted away as she watched him walk towards her, her heart beating that little bit faster the way it always had when he was around. He hadn't seen her yet, distracted by his travel companion. It gave her time to study this older version of the man she'd loved when they were both very different people. A world away from where she truly belonged.

His hair was longer than she remembered but remained as unruly as ever. His sun-kissed brown locks refused to be tamed, curling behind his ears and framing his tanned face. The dark scruff of his beard roughened the smooth jaw line hiding in the bristles and when those unfathomable brown eyes met hers she had to swallow down the sudden thirst she'd worked up. The physical changes were minimal but there was one huge difference in his life that would take some getting used to.

'Seth, Amy, welcome to Belle Crepuscolo.' She advanced towards them the way she would when meeting any foreign dignitaries or people of importance arriving in her country. With her arms raised in welcome, she kissed him on both cheeks, telling herself this was nothing out of the ordinary. She knew she was lying to herself when his beard rasped against her skin and the mere touch of him caused a total blood rush to her head.

'Thank you for the VIP treatment, Kaja. It is Kaja, isn't it? Or should I address you as Your Majesty?' There was a twinkle in his eye as he said it but also an underlying tang of bitterness in his tone. Understandable in the circumstances.

'Kaja's fine.' She kept the smile painted on her face as the small hint at her betrayal hit its mark on her conscience. There was so much she had to apologise for, to explain, but nothing would take away the hurt she'd undeniably caused him five years ago. The best she could do was make this stay as comfortable as possible for her visitors.

'Well, Kaja, we've had a lovely trip so far. Haven't we, Amy?' Seth turned his attention to the munchkin clinging onto his hand.

'I'm glad they took good care of you. Now, if you're ready, you'll be escorted to the palace. Would you like that, Amy?' Kaja hunched down to talk to the little girl, trying to make a friend but understanding that this must be overwhelming for her. She'd been dragged away from the only place she'd ever known and flown halfway across the world. It was natural the child should be wary.

Amy looked to her father for guidance on the matter and when he nodded his head, she copied him, her brown curls bobbing in agreement.

When Kaja extended her hand, the child accepted it, her little fingers curling around the stranger she was being urged to trust. Amy smiled up at her with eyes so much like Seth's, Kaja's heart felt as though it were being torn into tiny pieces. The four-year-old was a walking reminder that Seth had moved on from their relationship all too quickly.

Within a couple of months of her leaving he'd married and started a family. A life he'd offered to Kaja first, so it was her own fault he'd found someone else. When he'd proposed, he'd been offering her a commitment she'd realised too late she couldn't give in return. It had been the wake-up call she'd needed to snap out of the dream she'd been living in England with him. She wasn't anything like the woman she'd pretended to be to Seth or their work colleagues. Princess in her own country, she had responsibilities and duties she'd been avoiding in her quest for a normal life. As much as she'd wanted it, it was beyond her grasp. None of it real when she hadn't even confided her true identity to Seth. A betrayal so great she couldn't bring herself to tell him she'd lied to him from the moment they'd met.

She had no right to be jealous now when she'd fled England without giving him an explanation. She was lucky he'd been willing to even speak to her again. Never mind come all this way to do her a favour.

'I'm sorry to hear about your father...and your mother, of course.' It was Seth who addressed the reason for this reunion first. Although, it wasn't a conversation she particularly wanted to have in front of her security team, who were shadowing their journey to the exit.

Her mother's death from a heart attack soon after Kaja's return to her homeland was one more layer of guilt heaped upon her shoulders. She'd been so intent on living a 'normal' life she'd distanced herself from her family and lost precious time she could have spent with her mother. A regret she'd thought she could make up for by falling into line with the rest of the family and throwing herself into what was expected of her as a princess. Including marrying someone out of duty rather than love.

Kaja was sure it hadn't taken Seth too long to work out her true heritage from the ensuing press coverage of her mother's death, though she'd kept it from him and everyone else while living in Cambridge.

The unspoken *Why?* and the hurt she'd caused were blazing so brightly in his gaze she was forced to turn away.

'Thank you. I wasn't able to help my mother but I'm hoping you can do something to save my father.' After years of being on dialysis, her father's kidneys had failed. They were lucky that he hadn't had to go on a waiting list for a new organ when her brother had turned out to be a match and was willing to donate one of his kidneys. With Seth one of the UK's most esteemed transplant surgeons, he was the first person she'd thought of when the nephrologist had told them dialysis was no longer working.

She reminded herself that was why she had brought Seth here. Not to resolve old personal issues or pick up where they'd left off—if that were even a possibility. Which it wasn't.

'We can discuss the details later.' The tensing in Seth's jaw gave her chills. It would seem he hadn't forgiven or forgotten after all and why should he? In the intervening years she'd yet to come to terms with her actions at that time and the consequential events.

She nodded, knowing it was a conversation she couldn't avoid. Seth had come all this way to help her family and an explanation for running out on him was the least she could give him in return.

'Are you really a princess?' A tiny voice broke through the adult tension.

'I really am.' She was second in line to the throne of this principality after her father and brother but a four-year-old wouldn't be interested in the politics or boring small print of her position. In a little girl's eyes, at least, she had all the trappings of a fairy-tale princess. Of course, the reality was much different and less enchanting than the bedtime stories.

'Do you have a glass coach and a fairy godmother?' Clearly, Seth had no problem in letting his daughter believe in the fantasy, regardless of his own experience and knowledge that happy-ever-afters didn't exist.

'I'm afraid not. I wish I did but this is it.' They stepped out onto the pavement, the sun warming Kaja's skin again after the chill of the air-conditioned airport.

The white limousine with her chauffeur at the helm was a privilege she didn't take for granted after her years using public transport in England. Although it likely wouldn't impress this Cinderella-loving youngster as much as an enchanted pumpkin and mouse coachman.

'I suppose this will have to do.' Seth let out a long whistle.

Kaja was aware this wasn't the norm for most people and only served to highlight the differences in their worlds.

Isak, her cheery chauffeur, got out, tipped his cap, and opened the door for them to get into the car.

'If you can bear it… Alderisi Palace is a short distance from here.' She stood back to let her guests climb onto the back seat first, seeing Amy's eyes light up when she heard their destination. If she had been disappointed by meeting Kaja, hopefully her home for the next few weeks would better live up to expectation. At least trying to keep a small child entertained should distract her from the prospect of her brother and father's operations. Along with the man who'd be performing them.

Her personal security guard, Gunnar, was riding up front and Amy had chosen to sit on one of the long side seats in the rear, leaving her and Seth on the back seat. Despite the vast car interior she found the amount of secrets and ghosts wedged in around them suffocating.

Amy was humming to herself and dancing one of the dolls she'd pulled out from her backpack along the leather upholstery, completely oblivious to the rest of the world around her.

'I hope having Amy with me isn't causing you any inconvenience.' Seth leaned across to speak to her privately, his warm breath brushing her cheek the way his fingers used to right before he kissed her…

'No. Not at all,' she said much too loudly, and sprang back from further thoughts of his touch upon her.

'I don't have anyone else to take care of her. Gran passed away last month. Although she hadn't been able to watch her for some time. Alzheimer's,' he confided, letting that one word fill in all the details he failed to give her.

Finding out he had a daughter when she'd contacted him had come as a shock. She hadn't expected him to be frozen in time in their semi-detached house, waiting for her call, but having it confirmed he'd led another life after her still hurt. Especially when he had the one thing she could never have. A child.

Kaja hadn't had time to mope around after her lost love due to her mother's passing. Then she'd been determined to atone for the neglect of her family by throwing herself into the royal duties she'd avoided until then. She'd met Benedikt at a fundraiser for the public hospital where she worked in the emergency department once a week; a position she'd had to fight to keep hold of as some measure of independence. Although her brief working week meant she'd never really fitted into the hospital team as well as the one she'd worked with in England.

Benedikt had been older than her and from one of Belle Crepuscolo's wealthiest families. She'd believed marriage to him, becoming a power couple on the world's stage, would please her father, to whom family and tradition meant everything. That somehow a prestigious match would fill the void left by her mother and make up for the years she'd abandoned her post in her home country. Having a baby was part of that duty, to secure the family line and make her husband and father happy. Her failure to get pregnant and her spouse's philandering shattered that dream. Benedikt's affair and subsequent filing for divorce to marry his pregnant mistress had played out for the world to see and gossip about. Whereas Seth's life was a closed book to her. One she suddenly wanted to binge-read.

'I'm sorry to hear about your grandmother. I know you were close.'

'Yeah. Her and Gramps raised me as their

own. Now they've both gone I'm a bit lost, to be honest. I think the trip out here will do Amy some good to get away from my moping around.' His sad smile was one she could relate to, having lost her own mother and still having to function for other people's sake.

At a time when a person simply wanted to wallow and wail over the loss of someone important in their life, one had to plaster on a happy face for appearances' sake and pray it would stop everyone else falling apart too.

'I assume your wife couldn't get away to join you here?' She didn't imagine the child's mother would let her come out here unless she had other serious commitments preventing her from being with her daughter.

'Paula and I...er...aren't together any more. Haven't been for some time.'

'Sorry. I didn't know.' Once she'd heard he'd married so quickly after their separation she hadn't wanted to know any more. She'd simply accepted he'd moved on without her and taken steps to do the same. Something she'd later come to regret.

'Yes, well, Amy was the best thing to come out of that relationship.' His steely set jaw and change in his tone conveyed there were bad feelings lingering about the situation.

'You share custody?'

'No. Her mother left and never looked back. It's just the two of us now. That's the way we like it, isn't it, Ames?' The little girl nodded, though she couldn't have heard the nature of their conversation.

Kaja got the impression this was a mantra he repeated often so they'd both believe it.

'You certainly seem as though fatherhood is agreeing with you and she's gorgeous. A real credit to you.' She could see Seth as a single dad, braiding his daughter's hair and organising playdates. He'd always wanted children even though they'd both been busy with their careers. It was a topic she'd tried to avoid. She could see now that it was because she knew they would never have been able to settle down as a family. Not when she hadn't been honest with him about her background.

Ironic, when she probably couldn't have given him a baby anyway. Irregular periods and her failure to get pregnant with Benedikt had led to a diagnosis of polycystic ovaries and the end of her marriage. Not even the invasive laser treatment she'd undertaken to try and fix the problem could prevent her husband from straying.

Now Seth was a father she was certain Amy was top priority in his life. Despite his dedication to his profession and his patients, Seth always put his loved ones first. Unlike her. In looking out for her own interests Kaja had managed to hurt the man she'd loved and her family.

He'd looked after his grandparents in their old age and he'd been committed to her during their relationship. To the point of proposing marriage.

Now she'd invited Seth back into her life she was reminded of everything she'd lost when she came home.

'Thanks. It's not exactly how I saw my life panning out but I wouldn't be without her for the world.' The proud father confirmed what Kaja had already seen for herself in the short time since their arrival.

'You're lucky to have each other.' Seth was currently having a dolls' tea party in Amy's honour on the back seat of the limousine. Anyone could see they had a special bond. One she was quite envious of when she'd never get to have that close relationship with her own child.

Even if continued treatment meant she could conceive some day, it was a lot to go through without a guarantee of success. To her, love, marriage and children were all inextricably linked and Benedikt had proved that without one of those links everything else fell apart.

'You never thought of having kids yourself?' It was the sort of question adults asked each other all the time, catching up on each other's news after losing touch. Yet it touched a still exposed and very raw nerve.

'I thought about it. It just didn't work out for me.' Even saying that, reducing what she'd gone through to a vague disappointment brought forth a swell of sadness from the pit of her stomach threatening to swamp her. It was the ensuing anger that had accompanied that period that had prevented her from drowning in her sorrow altogether.

'I know you've had a rough time too.'

There. Her humiliation was complete to find Seth hadn't missed the spotlight shone on her own disastrous marriage, even if he wasn't party to the devastating details of her infertility problems.

'I never was very good at making those big

life decisions.' She'd wondered how differently her life would've turned out if she'd accepted his proposal and settled in England for good. Although, it wouldn't have solved the problem that had caused the end of her marriage. She'd loved him too much to ever force him into a future without the family he was born to have.

'We all make mistakes. What's important is that we learn to forgive ourselves, as well as each other.' He fixed her under his gaze, warm like melted chocolate. She hoped it was his way of telling her he'd forgiven her for her past mistakes. If they'd been somewhere more private, perhaps in better circumstances, she would've asked him for clarification and taken that as a cue to apologise. There'd be plenty of opportunity to do so over the course of the next few days when they'd be living under the same roof.

'That can be hard to do when you know you're the facilitator of your own downfall.' No one had forced her to leave Seth, marry someone she hardly knew or to stay in a country where she no longer garnered any respect. She'd managed that all by herself. It was no wonder she'd been given the dubious nickname of 'The Unlovable Princess' when it was such an accurate description.

'I don't think you have it as bad as you make out, Princess. You might take all this for granted but look around you. This is priceless.' Seth wasn't telling her anything she didn't know or showing her things she hadn't seen before. Although, as he leaned across her to direct her gaze out of the window, she wasn't inclined to tell him so. It was an age since she'd been this close to a man, *this* man, and she revelled in the warmth of his body and the masculine scent of sweat and cologne clinging to his skin.

Belle Crepuscolo, as the name suggested, was a beautiful country. Landlocked by Switzerland, Italy and Austria, it had an enviable climate and a culture influenced by all the surrounding countries.

While Seth watched the blur of blue skies and sprawling whitewashed villas flash by the window, Kaja was more interested in the view she had. Seth was more a sense of home to her than the vista outside and she realised everything she'd truly left behind in England that fateful day.

'There's more to life than money and sunshine. That old adage holds true. None of it can buy you happiness.' To her, privilege had become a prison. It kept her trapped in a life she was desperate to break free from.

Her happiest time had been during those rain-drenched, barely-time-to-sit-down working days in Cambridge. At least then she'd had Seth to come home to. They'd cooked dinner, curled up together in front of the telly and made love in their own bed. Nothing out of the ordinary and yet it had been everything. Being so close to him now reminded her of those cosy nights in when she'd been pretending she could lead a normal life. Before reality crashed in and reminded her it wasn't possible.

'That's easy to say when you have this on your doorstep. What else could you possibly want?' He turned his brilliant smile on her and she was powerless to hold her tongue or tell him anything but the truth.

'Love.'

She saw that spike of pain on his face before he composed himself and returned to his own side of the car. They both knew she'd had that once in her life and thrown it away. The Unlovable Princess deserved everything that had come to her since then.

Seth hadn't been as prepared to face Kaja as he'd thought. For some reason he'd thought he'd fly out here, do the job he was required to do and, once he'd seen her, all that past hurt and betrayal would melt away. He'd got it into his head that facing her would make him realise everything had turned out for the best. After all, if Kaja hadn't run out on him he wouldn't have slept with someone else on the rebound or had Amy as a consequence. While he regretted the hasty marriage, he'd never be sorry for his daughter's existence. She was his everything.

He'd known the minute he'd set eyes on Kaja again closure wasn't going to be achieved so easily. It didn't matter that five years had passed, that they'd both married, and divorced, since, or that he'd become a father. In that moment, seeing her again had transported him back to the day he'd proposed. When she'd rejected him, packed her bags in the middle of the night and disappeared without a trace. All the confusion and fear of that time was tied up in the memory. Along with the anger and sense of betrayal he'd felt when he'd seen her on the news as word of her mother's death had spread. A princess. He'd had no inkling of her heritage, couldn't imagine Kaja as anything other than his busy surgeon girlfriend. Until now.

She'd swapped her green scrubs and sneakers for pink silk and diamonds but she was as beautiful as ever. As though her fairy godmother had waved a magic wand and enhanced her natural beauty for the oblivious prince who'd needed it spelled out to him what an amazing woman she was. It was unfortunate her real Prince Charming had turned out to be anything but, according to the papers. Seth took no pleasure in reading about her heartache but perhaps there was something to be said for the commoner she'd snubbed after all. Seth had loved her for who she was, or, at least, who he'd believed she was, with no need for a substitute.

He knew what it was to be hurt and to think you were inadequate. After all, he'd been abandoned by a teenage mother who'd thought having a baby would ruin her life and a wife who'd pretty much thought the same about him and their daughter. Kaja hadn't even bothered to give him a reason why his love wasn't enough for her.

Despite their personal history, Kaja had deserved better than being cheated on. Just as he'd deserved better than being ghosted.

'I mean, when it comes down to health matters we're no better off than the average person. We can fly the best renal surgeon out here to perform the transplant but there's no guarantees my father and brother will survive. If anything happens to them I'll have no one left in my life.' Her voice broke. It was at odds with the cool composure she'd shown at the airport. He'd known in that instant she hadn't regretted her actions when she'd seemed so personally unmoved by seeing him again. Meanwhile his insides had been churning as though he'd hit turbulence even after he'd stepped off the plane.

For a split second he'd wondered if she'd missed him or what they'd had together. She'd quickly shut down that idea, letting him know it was her family she was getting emotional over. He should've known better. Kaja's family was all she'd cared about in the end. It was a pity he hadn't known about their existence until it had been too late to do anything.

'Hey, have a little faith in your transplant surgeon. Nothing's going to take them away from you. Besides, don't you have a whole country to keep you company?' Since his gran had passed he'd been more aware than ever of his limited social circle. With his time no longer eaten up talking to carers or visiting the home, outside work Amy was his whole world. While he was content with that, he knew it wasn't healthy for a four-year-old. Before that cruel disease had robbed her of cognitive thought, Gran herself had made him swear to get a life of his own after she'd gone. To take Amy to see the world and have adventures.

Kaja's call for help had been a well-timed gift, an easier way out than forging new friendships in a place where he'd happily existed on the periphery of society. His busy life as a renal transplant and general surgeon made it challenging to balance work and home life. As a result any thoughts of another romantic relationship had gone on the back burner in favour of spending time with his daughter and grandmother when he could. Now he'd packed up and fled the country with his daughter so he didn't have to face life without the woman who'd been the only constant in his life. This trip had been the cowardly way out of his grief and he knew that sense of loss would be waiting for him on his return.

Kaja might be feeling sorry for herself now but she had no idea what it truly meant to be abandoned by the ones you loved. He'd been abandoned by his own mother and wife. Whereas she was the one who did the abandoning.

Kaja disputed his take on her life with a, 'Hah!'

'Daddy, look!' Amy was straining to see out of the window. He leaned over to see what had caught her attention.

His mouth dropped open as they drove up a winding avenue lined with blush-pink cherry blossoms and crystal-clear dancing water fountains.

'Home, sweet home,' Kaja mocked as the imposing mansion at the end of the drive came into view.

Gleaming white stone pillars, marble steps and balconies on every level of the ornate building gave it the appearance of a grand, layered wedding cake. A congregation of immaculately dressed people spilled out to meet the car. Seth immediately unbuckled Amy's seat belt and took her hand so she didn't get lost in the throng.

'Baby, we're not in Cambridge any more.'

CHAPTER TWO

'I'LL GET THAT for you, sir.'

'Let me take your bag for you, sir.'

The car had barely come to a halt before there was a flurry of helping hands refusing to let Seth so much as open the door on his own. He clutched Amy closer in case she was spirited away by Kaja's staff with his luggage.

'Hold my hand so you don't get lost, sweetheart.'

'I suppose it is all rather much.' Kaja winced.

It hadn't been his intention to make her self-conscious about her life here. She must have preferred it to the one they'd had together as she'd left it behind so readily.

If they were going to spend the next few weeks under the same roof they were going to have to get along. All issues—personal or socio-economic—would have to be set aside in order for him to treat her father. His patients' backgrounds were none of his business unless it impacted on their health. From everything he'd seen so far, Kaja's father had the best of everything money could buy. Including health care. However, his status wasn't going to affect Seth's ability to do his job. He always did his best regardless of wealth or the status of his patients.

'I'm sure we'll get used to it.' He flashed her a grin. Reassurance that they could make this work. It was his duty to put the minds of his patients' family members at ease where he could. Even if these were unusual circumstances.

'Daddy? Can we have a sleepover in the princess castle?' Amy tugged on his shirt, her eyes wide as she took in the majesty, the likes of which he'd only seen in picture books.

'See?' he said to Kaja with a laugh. 'I think we'll fit in just fine.'

'Good. Why don't we go in and I'll show you to your rooms.' The worry lines marring her forehead evened out into a smile matching his daughter's.

Now that the palace staff had disappeared inside with his belongings it was slightly less intimidating. At least, until they walked through the doors.

The 'wow' escaped his lips before he could temper his reaction. It was difficult to say anything else when faced with the sheer opulence of the décor within the palace.

The rich purple and silver colour scheme combined with the draped silks and brightly coloured tapestries lining the walls was how he imagined the genie's pad inside the magic lamp looked.

When the imposing oak door swung shut, echoing through the halls, it made the situation very real. The heavyset dude who shadowed Kaja's every move without saying a word remained on the outside acting as a sentry.

'Your apartments are this way.'

Not room, he noted as Kaja led them up a flight of steps to the 'apartments'.

'There is an elevator should you wish to use it but I prefer to take the stairs otherwise I'd never get any exercise.'

The Kaja he'd known would've been bored rigid at being chauffeured everywhere, barely allowed to lift a finger. Like him, she'd been someone who'd thrived on being busy, being needed, and had enjoyed her privacy. The alone time they'd spent together had been more precious than he'd realised.

'I don't think you have anything to worry about on that score.' He could see she'd lost weight and some of her curves but none of her beauty. She had an elegant grace about her now befitting a princess. That look-don't-touch vibe was so different from the warm, tactile Kaja he'd planned to marry.

She paused on the steps with her hand resting on the mahogany bannister and slowly turned to look back at him. It was then he realised her backside had been in his eyeline when he'd made that last comment, and he attempted to backtrack.

'I mean, I'm sure you get a workout simply moving from one room to another in here. A few circuits sprinting up and down these steps every morning will help keep me in shape too.' It wasn't a total lie to cover his tracks. He'd let his gym membership lapse when he'd been busy running between Amy's childcare and Gran's nursing home. He'd have to begin a fitness regime when the hospitality thus far had been so effectively displayed. Getting fed around here didn't seem as though it was going to be a problem. Especially when there were silver dishes piled high with juicy citrus fruit and pastel-coloured almonds dotted around the palace at regular intervals.

'Uh-huh.' Kaja gave him a disbelieving look then carried on up the staircase.

Amy broke away from him, sprinting on up to reach the landing first. Not waiting for the adults to catch up, she bolted down the corridor, giddy at having so much space to go wild in after being cooped up in a plane for so long.

'Amy, keep the noise down and don't touch anything.' He had visions of her bursting in on an unsuspecting dignitary and causing an international incident as she treated the place like her own. A child her age had no comprehension of the complex relationships going on around her. Only the scope of the place for potential fun and mischief. Seth didn't know if Kaja understood what she was in for hosting his daughter.

'Oh, don't worry. You're the only ones on this floor apart from me and the staff. She won't disturb anyone. Bruno and father are already at the private hospital where you'll be working. I'll take you to see them later. I'm sure you and Amy would appreciate some time to settle in first.'

'Thanks. That's very kind of you. I think a nap might be in order.'

'No problem. I know at your age you need all the sleep you can get.'

The jibe caught him off guard, as did the mischievous grin she was sporting. It was a glimpse back at the girl who'd teased him constantly about being a whole three years older and of the close relationship they'd once had.

'Ha, ha. I was thinking more of Amy.' He would never admit the day had taken its toll on him as well, albeit on a more emotional level than he'd anticipated. If Kaja remained unaffected by his presence after all these years as she seemed, there was no point in letting her know he still had unresolved feelings surrounding their past.

He'd only jumped into the relationship with Paula because he'd been so desolate without Kaja and he'd needed someone to provide the company, the intimacy he'd lost with her gone. In hindsight he could see that by rushing headlong into that relationship he'd opened himself up to further rejection from Paula. They hadn't known each other long enough to survive a pregnancy and a marriage so soon after meeting. Perhaps he'd been so keen for the family he'd pictured with Kaja he'd transferred those dreams unfairly onto his spouse. In some way perhaps he'd also wanted to prove his absent mother wrong, prove that it was possible to have a successful career and children. And that someone could love him and want him in their life. Though as of now, the only person who did was his daughter.

'Of course you were…' She patted him on the shoulder with the tease but he noticed the flare of panic in her eyes when she realised what she was doing and snatched her hand away again. It was too late for him to forget her touch now he had physical proof this wasn't a dream and she was real after all.

'Now, this is where you will be staying.' She snapped back into courteous hostess mode and opened the ornately carved oak door etched with leaves and flowers, leading to a suite so big Seth feared he'd lost Amy already. The gold and cream colour scheme wasn't easy on the eyes as it screamed money. Along with not being childproof.

'Just us? I'm sure we could fit in a few more single-parent families if you wanted to open this up as a holiday retreat.' He wasn't trying to be facetious but this one room would swallow up his entire house and still leave enough space to build another.

Kaja ignored the comment, picked up a porcelain bell from the glass table just inside the door and gave it a tinkle. Immediately, one of the staff he'd seen outside appeared in the doorway.

'This is Nils. If you need anything ring the bell. He's here to assist you in any way he can.'

'I really don't think that'll be necessary.' He wasn't aware how long it had taken Kaja to get used to having people running around after her but he was sure it was longer than a few weeks.

His home with Kaja in Cambridge had once been their oasis away from the outside world. A private place to be themselves away from the stresses of hospital life and people who wanted something from them. That hadn't changed for him. He was still in the same house and it remained his safe haven. No matter how luxurious Kaja's residence was, he wasn't going to trade his and Amy's privacy to take advantage of the perks offered.

He couldn't imagine Kaja slobbing around in her PJs here on a day off, eating cereal out of the box and binge-watching her favourite TV shows. Mind you, he couldn't see this perfectly polished princess knowing how to chill out at all any more.

'It's no trouble at all, sir. I'm at your disposal.' The deferential bow didn't go any way to assuaging Seth's discomfort at having someone at his personal beck and call.

'I think that will be all for now, Nils.' Kaja dismissed her employee on his behalf. It was disconcerting to find she could summon this impressive male specimen at the mere ring of a bell. Although Kaja's personal life was nothing to do with him any more. He was here in a professional capacity. To perform a life-saving operation, then get the hell out of fantasy land and back to the real world.

'Seth, I know you value your privacy but you're going to need help. With Amy, at least. It's not a comment on your character to accept some assistance. Think of it as a perk.'

'Daddy, come and see my room. It's got toys and everything.' Amy appeared and grabbed him by the hand, tugging him away from Kaja and any chance of a meaningful conversation.

'We got a few things in to make your stay more enjoyable. I'll arrange transport over to the hospital when you're ready. Amy is welcome to help herself to the toys.'

'I appreciate you going to all this trouble for us.' She'd gone to a lot of effort to make them comfortable. Some might say too much. He couldn't help but think it was due to a guilty conscience and was beginning to wish they'd booked into a hotel instead.

Kaja excused herself and left the room. With the door closed behind her, separating her from Seth and Amy, she let out a long, ragged breath. Seeing him again was never going to be a straightforward meet and greet when theirs had been much more than a professional acquaintance. She'd known that. Yet, she hadn't been prepared for the tumultuous emotions seeing him again would churn up.

Her entire adult life seemed to flash before

her eyes in the short time since they'd been re-acquainted. All the mistakes she'd made, the regrets, and, almost worst of all, the good times she'd had with Seth, came flooding into her brain. Cuddled up together back then, there'd been none of this awkward formality she'd adopted to protect her status in her home country and her heart.

When she'd heard he had a daughter he intended to bring with him it was undeniable evidence that Seth had been in another serious relationship. A marriage no less. Except Amy, the spitting image of her father, was completely adorable and Kaja had fallen in love with her the second she'd taken her hand.

Now it was going to be doubly hard not to get personally involved with her house guests. The sooner she got Seth settled at the hospital to oversee her father's kidney transplant, the better. Then her whole focus would be on her family's survival.

'Is everything all right, ma'am?'

'Yes, Fatima. I'm going to retire to my quarters now. Perhaps you could bring me some tea.'

'Right away.' Her faithful lady-in-waiting was

more of a friend and a confidante, the only person Kaja could talk to, but when it came down to it, Fatima was paid to listen. Just as Seth was being paid to be here. It appeared the richer she was, the higher status she had, the lonelier she became. She didn't want to be alone in her ivory tower any more and would give anything to be back in England where she'd had work colleagues, friends, neighbours and a loving boyfriend. But she'd given it all up to do her duty to her country and could never go back.

Even here in her own home she couldn't simply take a duvet day for some time out of her duties. There were always people coming and going, expecting an audience with her without offering any real, personal interaction. She also had an image to maintain, if only in the presence of the palace staff. Sometimes she wondered if Seth was the only one who'd ever truly known her but she hadn't been honest with him either about who she was or where she'd come from.

Now he knew the truth, Seth would see right through her to how unhappy she was in this life she'd left him for. It was karma, she supposed, for what she'd put him through. Not only had she lied to him but she'd abandoned Seth and the life they'd had together as though it were nothing. The truth was it had been everything.

CHAPTER THREE

'FATIMA'S GOING TO mind you while Daddy's at work. I'll see you when I get back, okay?' Seth kissed his baby on the top of her head then joined Kaja at the front door.

'She'll be fine, Mr Davenport. Amy and I have this whole house to play in. We can make some cookies for everyone to enjoy later too.' Fatima separated the clingy youngster from her father's trouser leg.

'You'll enjoy that, Amy. Fatima makes the best cookies in the country.' When she had free time, Kaja helped Fatima bake too. It took her mind off matters outside the kitchen and she got to comfort eat afterwards.

While it didn't help maintain her trim waistline, whipping up a few biscuits went a long way to clearing the clutter from her mind. Worries, memories, regrets—it was better to bake them in the oven than spend another night locked away in a room with them.

'I'll see you later, sweetie.' Seth gave Amy one last hug then Fatima distracted her with one of the new toys they'd bought so she wouldn't fret after him—a bright yellow convertible car to drive her dolls around in was just the thing to draw her attention.

'If there are any problems, call me. You've got my phone number, right?'

'Yes, Mr Davenport.' Fatima was smiling but she probably just wanted them to leave so she could get on with taking care of her charge. She loved children and helped raise Kaja and Bruno. They'd preferred her company over any of the nannies their parents had ever employed and she'd become like their second mum. As someone who'd devoted her life to looking after others, the prospect of spending the day with an excitable four-year-old was undoubtedly preferable to her usual housework routine.

'Don't worry. The Royal Alderisi Hospital is only five minutes down the road.' There were some advantages to ruling such a small country and having access to the best health care money could buy was one of them.

She led Seth outside where the afternoon sunshine cast a golden glow on everything it

touched, illuminating the immaculately mani-
cured gardens and showing off her country in
the very best light.

'Can't we walk? It's a beautiful day and, well,
I'm finding everything a little stifling in there.'

Kaja understood. Between the staff, and
their history waiting patiently to be unpicked,
it was claustrophobic. There was barely room to
breathe despite the size of the place. However,
when you were royalty simple things such as
a walk alone weren't possible. Another thing
she missed about England, where people were
too busy, too involved in their own lives to be
concerned with hers.

'Sorry.' She shrugged, continuing to apologise for the way she ran her life here. 'It's a security issue. With the amount of preparation it
would take in advance, it's quicker and easier
to take the car. Perhaps we can work something
out for tomorrow.'

Seth sighed and approached the limo already
waiting for them with the doors open and the
chauffeur readied. He'd obviously tired of the
regime after only a couple of hours but seeing
it might help him understand why she'd left in
the first place and moved to Cambridge.

'It doesn't matter. I'm being a nuisance. It'll take a bit of time to get used to things here, that's all. You don't have to keep apologising for everything.' He gestured for her to get into the car first and once the door closed she wished that walk were a possibility. Now there was no escape from confronting their troubled history.

'Don't I?' If she said sorry every day for the entire time he was here it wouldn't be enough to cancel out the wrong she'd done him.

'It's your life. You shouldn't have to apologise for the way you live. I'm only here in a professional capacity after all.' He'd sat at the opposite end from her on the back seat. For all her worry about being enclosed in here with him, now she wanted to close some of that emotional distance that had settled between them.

'That's not strictly true, is it? I got you here to carry out my father's kidney transplant because I know you're the best, but it would be remiss of me not to address what happened five years ago.'

'I don't want to drag that up and cause any ill feeling that might impact on the job I'm here to do.' Seth's attempt to evade the subject only succeeded in making Kaja feel worse by admitting there was lingering resentment on his part. She didn't want to create a toxic environment at the hospital, or in her home, but neither did she want to keep acting as though they were strangers. In her opinion it was better to get things out and clear the air instead of tiptoeing around each other faking congeniality.

'That's why I thought it best to tackle it now and explain myself. It's the least you deserve.'

He didn't argue any further, proving her right. She took a deep breath and settled her hands in her lap in the hope they would stop shaking.

'I should have told you about my family from the start. I am sorry about that.' Along with everything else, but apologies couldn't alter history.

'Why didn't you, Kaja? We had a life together. I thought I knew who you were.' When he did look at her the pain shining so brightly in his eyes took her breath away. All this time she'd convinced herself he'd got over her was rendered a convenient lie when he was clearly still so affected by her actions.

'You've got to understand, Seth, I went to England to escape my life here. I never envisaged anything beyond that. After graduating high school I was expected to take on my own royal duties and projects. A scary prospect for an eighteen-year-old who wanted to be like everyone else. I persuaded my parents that getting a medical degree would be useful to my position when I returned. That I could put it to good use in the community. I told them England was the best place to study. Where no one knew me. Selfishly, I chose it because it was so far away I reckoned I was beyond their reach. They couldn't make me go back. As time went on I created a life there and I met you. I lived, studied and worked there so long I didn't think my heritage mattered any more. I didn't tell you the truth about who I was because I was in denial myself. I had no intention of coming back.'

'Until I asked you to marry me. Then you disappeared without a trace.'

She hung her head, not knowing how she could begin to make amends for her cowardice. 'That was my wake-up call. My reminder that I was living in a bubble with you. You weren't asking a lot except for a normal, family life. Something you would've found with anyone other than me. There's nothing normal about my family or my life, as you can see, but you're right, I shouldn't have gone like that. You deserved better.'

'Yes, I did.' He clearly wasn't going to make this easy for her.

'Your proposal made me realise I was fooling myself in living out this fantasy I could marry you and simply be Mrs Davenport. I had obligations at home that would have caught up with me eventually and I thought it best to end things before I entered into a marriage based on lies.' The right thing to do, evidently, when she couldn't have helped him realise his dream of becoming a father either.

'You could have told me that. I'd rather have talked things over than wake up to find you'd gone.'

'I panicked, didn't know where to begin explaining myself and thought I could do it better from a distance. I intended to get in contact but then my mother died and I was swept away in a tidal wave of grief.'

'You could have at least got a message to me.'

Even with the air conditioning on Kaja was feeling the heat, shame burning her from the inside out. 'I was a mess, Seth. I was grieving for my mother, and feeling guilty for everything I'd put everyone through. Believe it or not I thought by leaving I was somehow saving you from getting hurt too instead of stringing you along pretending to be someone I wasn't.'

Seth's soulless laugh disputed her warped sense of logic. 'How did you work that one out when you didn't explain any of that to me? Didn't you think I'd be worried that something had happened to you when you vanished without a trace? For all I knew you could've been abducted or had some sort of accident. I called everyone we knew and the hospitals and police. Of course, when they heard you'd rejected my marriage proposal they decided it was your way of dumping me. It took me a little longer to work things out.'

'I'm sorry.' Her voice came out as small as she felt right now. She'd never meant to humiliate him but she was guilty of thinking only about herself. In her attempt to avoid a confrontation or get talked into staying, she'd jumped on the next flight without thinking about the impact her disappearance would have on him.

He didn't need to know that her fertility issues had helped her to maintain that distance since. There hadn't seemed a need to reach out to him when there was no chance of a happy-ever-after and so she had only done so when her father's survival was at stake. It was a private matter she didn't have to share with anyone because she had no plans on repeating past mistakes. Getting involved with anyone would only bring heartache and pain when she could never live up to expectation. She had reconciled herself to never having children, perhaps never being in another relationship, because experience had shown her it wasn't feasible. That didn't mean she didn't yearn for both of those things. More so now that Seth was here, representing everything she wanted and couldn't have.

'When I saw you on the news at your mother's funeral I thought I was hallucinating. Never mind that you'd told me both your parents had died a long time ago, there you were walking behind your mother's coffin with your father, the grand duke.' He shook his head as though he was still trying to come to terms with it all.

'What can I do to fix things between us, Seth? I don't want you to hate me.'

'I could never hate you, Kaja, that's half of

the problem. What's done is done, I suppose. We can't change what's happened so there's no point in dwelling on it. I don't think I'll ever forget but I can learn to forgive.' The smile he gave her was devastating on so many levels it made her want to weep. The fact that this man she'd obviously wounded deeply had been willing to fly halfway around the world to help her family and forgive her showed the strength of his character compared to hers.

There were other questions she had about his life but this was more than she could ever have asked of him. Anything else she needed to say to him could wait. It was more important that they started out on this journey on amicable terms when these next few days were going to be tough. A kidney transplant was no small operation. It came with risks to everyone involved. She was putting her faith in Seth to get them all through this and that would be easier to do with the knowledge he didn't hold a grudge against her.

'Thanks.' It seemed inadequate to express how grateful she was for everything he was doing for her when he would've been within his rights to refuse to even take her call. For now, it was the best she could give him. It probably wouldn't improve relations between them if she burst into tears and told him leaving him was the biggest mistake she'd ever made in her life.

They were going to have plenty of time together as her family members went through this huge procedure and, hopefully, she'd be able to show him just how sorry she was about ending their relationship. Maybe then they'd both find some closure.

Seth was glad the journey wasn't too long between the palace and the hospital. Kaja's attempt to call a truce so they could move on had actually caused them to lapse into an even more uncomfortable silence. One only broken when they reached their destination and she advised him on the proper protocol for meeting her father. He found it disconcerting being in this alien situation when she'd been a huge part of his life for so long. A woman he'd been so comfortable around once upon a time.

With their conversation slipping back onto more familiar, albeit rockier, ground he'd almost forgotten he was dealing with royalty. He suspected etiquette would be more scrutinised by her father.

As it was, he was glad he hadn't tried to gain access to the hospital, or his patients, alone. A stranger's face didn't seem welcome as they were met with imposing guards at every corner.

'Isn't this a tad OTT? As far as I'm aware your country doesn't have a high crime rate, never mind a history of assassination attempts. I thought your family was more of a figurehead than a political party?' He'd done his home-work. Not only did the country have a ban on personally held firearms, with the exception of the military and police, they had one of the lowest crime rates in the world. From every-thing he'd read the population was pretty con-tent here since most residents had their own wealth and status. It was a tax haven for the rich and famous after all, as well as those born into a booming economy.

The royal family appeared popular even if the articles he'd skimmed concerning Kaja's love life were less than complimentary. He knew she'd abhor the constant attention and the patronising, cruel nickname the press had awarded her.

She spoke in her own language to another of the guards who'd attempted to block their access down the corridor. Another reminder he no longer knew the woman beside him when he'd been unaware English wasn't her mother tongue. He could only assume the gist of the conversation was something along the lines of, 'Don't you know who I am?', given Kaja's stern body language and the chided guard stepping back to let them pass. He continued to glare at Seth as they passed, perhaps unconvinced about his credentials rather than his companion's.

'We can't afford to take any chances. The whole world knows where my brother and father are. You can't expect us to let people swan in and out as they choose.'

Apart from the extra staff, it looked like any other private hospital Seth had worked in. It was clean and airy, with the extra touches of artwork on the walls and aquariums lit up with brightly coloured marine life setting it apart from the facilities attended by lesser mortals.

In his experience the added luxury of comfortable beds in private rooms or in-house chefs serving up specially tailored meals didn't mean a lot in the grand scheme of things. It wouldn't matter if the walls were made of pure gold or the floors were encrusted with diamonds. At the end of the day he was employed to do the same job he did everywhere else. Money couldn't buy a clean bill of health.

Kaja knew that. Perhaps that was why she was so on edge. She could fly someone out with the best surgical reputation in the world to perform this transplant but the rest of the recovery was down to fate. There was a possibility her father could reject the new organ. As always, Seth would do everything he could to prevent that happening but there were no guarantees in this life. He'd found that out for himself the hard way.

Another guard outside her father's private room greeted their arrival with a curt nod of the head, followed by a conversation on his walkie-talkie before they gained admittance. Seth assumed his face was on an all points bulletin by now, his whole background undergoing a thorough check if it hadn't already. He prayed his recent site visits to research the country— the ones about their princess in particular—

wouldn't come back to haunt him if they looked into his online search history.

'Father, this is Seth Davenport. The surgeon who's carrying out your transplant.' Kaja stood in the centre of the large private room announcing him to the frail gentleman swamped in his bed by pristine white cotton sheets and plump pillows.

'Ah, come forward, young man. My eyes aren't what they used to be. Along with the rest of me.' The grand duke sat up, immediately adopting an air of authority, which forced Seth to advance from the doorway towards the bed.

'I'm honoured to meet you, Your Royal Highness.' Seth dipped at the waist into a bow as prompted by Kaja, secretly hoping he wasn't expected to do this every time he walked into the room. It would become tiresome when he had a job to do.

The grand duke waved a dismissive hand. 'We can dispense with all of that nonsense. Call me Olov. I fear it is I who should be bowing to you. I can't thank you enough for coming to our little corner of the world to help me. My daughter tells me you once worked together and that you're the best there is.'

His excellent English was heavily accented compared to Kaja's. Seth assumed it was the time she'd spent in Cambridge studying that had made her sound more like a local.

It was clear she hadn't shared their personal history with her family. The grand duke might not have been so humble and welcoming if he'd known Seth had lived in sin with his only daughter for years, or that he'd had the audacity to propose marriage to her. Now he'd seen her life out here and the people she was surrounded by it was becoming clearer why she wouldn't entertain the idea of marrying a commoner like him. What more could he have possibly offered her that she didn't have already? Nothing except his love. Which hadn't been enough for her to even stay in the same country.

'That's correct, sir.' He wasn't going to be modest about his credentials when that was the reason he was here. Kaja's father would expect confidence from the man who would have his life in his hands.

'Good. At least something positive came out of Kaja's time away.' The focus of both men's attention lowered her head. Seth didn't know if it was in deference to her father or because she couldn't look at him.

Goodness only knew what she'd told her father about her career or her personal life during that time. It was a punch in the gut to think that their life together was nothing for her to be proud of when they'd been some of the best days of his life. Along with some of the worst after she'd gone.

'I've read up on your medical history and your nephrologist's recommendations. As far as I can see the procedure should be relatively straightforward.' Seth adopted his professional persona, determined not to linger on anything liable to distract him from the upcoming surgery.

'Glad to hear it. The last thing I want is to find out there could be more complications or setbacks. Time's running out for me.'

Seth didn't argue with him. He'd read the files and agreed that the transplant was the last option available given his condition. If he'd been any older or less fit than he was, a transplant might've been deemed too risky.

'This kind of operation comes with its own risks. We can't predict how your body will react to the transplanted organ. Obviously, we'll be monitoring you very closely and will do everything we can to prevent rejection. I'll need to meet with the rest of the team to discuss contingency plans to cover every eventuality.' Although he was the medical lead he wouldn't be able to do this without a team of other professionals with the same goal of making this operation a success.

'I can organise that for you.'

He'd forgotten Kaja was in the room until she voiced her intention to help.

'I'd appreciate that.'

'Is there anything else you need me to do?'

Seth knew only too well how it felt to be powerless as your world continued to spin out of control and there was nothing you could do to halt it. Yet, her suggestion to contribute fell flat when it had been made clear to him it was only the present that interested her. With no real consideration towards him or their history.

'Not at the moment. If that changes I'll let you know.' He turned his back on her, doing his best to block her out of his head so he could think straight.

'What do you require from me, Doctor?

Apart from my kidney?' Another male voice entered the fray. Followed, of course, by another shadow figure who was quietly dismissed at the door.

Even if the new arrival hadn't been wearing an identical hospital gown to the one Kaja's father was sporting, the family likeness was uncanny. All three Alderisis had the same sea-green eyes, aquiline nose and height befitting royalty.

He held out a hand towards Seth. 'Bruno. Pleased to meet you.'

'Seth Davenport,' he countered as strong fingers gripped his in a handshake.

'This is my big brother. Bruno, this is the surgeon who'll be carrying out the transplant.' Kaja introduced them in case there was any doubt about their identities.

'Ah. So you're the man who'll be cutting me open and rummaging about in my insides?' The dark humour he employed wasn't unheard of in these situations. A lot of patients joked to cover their fears. Bruno did seem relaxed about the impending operation considering the sacrifice he was about to undertake to save his father.

'Bruno, I wish you would take this seriously.' Kaja chastised him with a clip around the ear.

'Don't tease your sister. You know how she worries,' the elder Alderisi scolded.

It was clear this was a family who cared deeply for one another. He had no idea why Kaja had found it necessary to keep them hidden from him during the course of their relationship. Yes, her heritage had come as a shock but he would've got over it given time.

'I am taking this seriously. Trust me, giving away one of my kidneys isn't something I would do on a whim.'

'If it's any comfort, donors have the same life expectancy, general health and kidney function as anyone else.' He said it as much for Kaja and Olov's benefit as Bruno's.

'See, Kaja? I trust my new best friend here not to botch this when he comes so highly recommended. I'm going to be under anaesthetic so I'm not the one who'll be doing the worrying.' A meaty hand slapped Seth on the back. He liked this guy. His whole attitude and demeanour was a refreshing change from the earlier heavy-hitting conversation he'd had with his sister.

'We will need you to fill in the consent forms and other necessary paperwork before we proceed.' If anything did go wrong, it was necessary to have everything down in writing to protect all those involved. They all knew the risks but Seth would be the one primarily shouldering responsibility or blame if necessary.

'No problem. It's not as though we have much else to do while we're waiting. We've exhausted the whole board-game collection and I don't think Father is up to a game of table tennis just yet. Maybe in a week or two when he's fully recovered with a new lease of life, thanks to my young, highly sought-after vital organs.'

Kaja rolled her eyes and groaned. 'I give up.'

'I'll arrange everything once I've had a meeting with the team. The paperwork, that is, not the table tennis.' Seth exchanged grins with the handsome prince, satisfied they were both on the same wavelength. It was a serious procedure but a positive one if everything went to plan.

'Good stuff. I can jot kidney transplant into my diary for this week, then?'

'I don't see why not once we have everything in place. I'll go back and check on my daughter and return later to go over any questions you think of in the interim.' He was keen to find out how Amy was getting on. He'd be spending a lot of these next few days at the hospital and wanted to spend as much time with Amy as he could now.

'I'll call for the car and get Isak to take us back to the palace.' Kaja motioned for the attention of the guards at the window.

'If you don't mind, I'd rather walk. I'm sure I don't need an entourage to keep me safe and I'd much rather get some fresh air.' Along with some distance from Kaja and the memories he couldn't quite manage to shut out altogether.

CHAPTER FOUR

'I LOVE YOU, BRU. I love you too, Papa.' Kaja struggled to say goodbye and leave them in the hands of the surgical team even though she knew it was for the best. They were the only family she was ever going to have.

She couldn't bear the thought of losing either of them but her father's age and health were against him. Despite that, she managed to stem the emotions welling up inside her. The last thing they needed to see was her crying before they went under the anaesthetic.

'You'd think we weren't coming back to hear you, sis.' Trust Bruno to be making jokes even at a time like this. Her father simply raised his hand to give a wave as though he were simply popping to one of his lengthy state dinners.

'Don't worry. They'll be back on the ward before you know it.' Seth met her at the door, already prepped in his surgical scrubs. It was the most he'd spoken to her in days, his time split between his patients and his apartments. He hadn't sought her out at all.

Of course, he had a lot of meetings with the rest of the transplant team to occupy him, but she thought he'd gone out of his way to avoid her since his introduction at the hospital to her family. Perhaps it was being faced with the reality of life here and the patients he'd agree to take on or down to her completely disregarding their life together in England as purely work-related. Although she didn't think either of them would have wanted to bring up their painful romantic history right before Seth performed the transplant. There didn't seem any need.

The truth was she'd never spoken to her father about her life in England. She didn't think it was necessary to rehash it all and detract from the work she'd come back to do. He didn't need to know about her disastrous love life now she was back in her rightful place at the palace. Except of course it wasn't that easy for her to forget.

It might have been different had her mother still been alive. She would've had someone to confide in, a female shoulder to cry on. As it was, she only had Fatima and she'd had to draw a line somewhere between friend and employee.

'This is going to be a very long day. As the donor, Bruno will go into Theatre first for the laparoscopic donor nephrectomy.'

'It's a less invasive procedure than the old method so that means a quicker recovery period, right?' Despite her own medical knowledge, she needed Seth's reassurance that they weren't taking unnecessary risks by going ahead with this surgery. He was the expert and could be more objective on the matter when it wasn't his own family he was dealing with.

'Yes. There'll be a few tiny incisions and we'll remove the kidney with the scope camera and miniaturised surgical instruments. It's a straightforward procedure I've been involved in on many occasions.'

'I know this is the best thing for my father but I can't help worrying about them both and what this means for the future.'

'A kidney from a living donor does give better long-term results and from a family member there are lower risks of complications or rejection. We hope for a better early function this way. You know all this, Kaja.'

She could detect his frustration with her, perhaps taking it personally that she had doubts about this transplant being a success. It wasn't Seth's abilities she was wary of but that possibility of losing another family member.

'I'm just trying to get things clear in my head. Perhaps I could watch you carry out the transplant?' She needed to do something to feel part of what was happening. If anything did go wrong then she would know she'd done her best too. She couldn't live with the extra guilt if she failed anyone else she loved.

'Honestly, I don't think that's a good idea. My advice would be to leave the hospital grounds for a while and find a distraction.'

'I couldn't do that. They need me here. I could just stay here—' She tried to go back into the room where her brother and father were keeping each other company before they went for surgery. Seth caught her none-too-gently by the elbow and pulled her back.

'Kaja, will you please just leave and let me get on with my job?'

Her mouth flopped open and closed at the audacity of Seth basically calling her a nuisance. Telling her she could be no help to her family and only a hindrance to him. It illustrated how far apart they'd drifted in the space of a couple of days. There was no way he spoke like this to any other anxious family members he encountered at work or she would've heard about it a long time ago. Colleagues had only ever said good things about him. It seemed this level of brusqueness had been reserved solely for her and it wasn't an honour she was enjoying.

As if she weren't tense enough already, Seth's sudden bout of control-freakery set her teeth on edge and her blood pressure rising.

'I'd prefer you kept our personal issues out of this, Seth. This isn't about you, or us, for that matter. You have no right to deny me access to my own family.'

'I don't want to call security to have you removed from the premises for being disruptive but I will if I have to.' Seth didn't acknowledge the accusation that he was exercising his authority in a vendetta against her. Which riled her even more.

'Disruptive to whom?' As if she didn't know.

'We'll phone you to let you know when they're out of surgery so you can visit. Okay?'

He seemed to soften a little towards her even if he wasn't backing down.

Kaja nodded. There seemed little point in arguing further and causing a scene. Especially when this was the man carrying out the transplant. She didn't want him going in to surgery distracted. They could hash this out at another time.

She hurried back to her waiting car giving no thought to Gunnar running to keep up with her, or Isak, who'd been snacking in the front seat. It didn't matter a jot she had to open her own door when she simply wanted somewhere to hide her tears, emotions catching up with her all at once.

'Take me home,' she commanded shakily and pushed the button to raise the privacy screen between her and her staff.

Only then was she safe to demonstrate her fragility. The tears didn't take time to fall once they started, streaking down her face as though someone had released a pressure valve and years of upset and turmoil had finally been allowed to be expressed. It was grief for her mother and the relationship with Seth she'd lost. Worry over her father and brother. Most of all it was sorrow for the life she'd been denied with Seth. If circumstances hadn't conspired against her she could've had a lifetime of being his wife instead of the half-life she had here as The Unlovable Princess no one wanted.

Seth wasn't proud of the way he'd spoken to Kaja but he needed her to be away from him while he operated on her father. He had to concentrate on what he was doing rather than worrying about what she was going through waiting for him to finish. As her anxiety had increased so too had his want to comfort her. That would have undone his efforts to put some distance between them these past few days and only brought them closer.

He'd succeeded in alienating her now and would be lucky if she forgave him for his behaviour at all. Regardless that he'd thought sending her home would be best for both of them. Kaja sitting here watching, worrying and waiting wasn't going to help anyone. Seth was the one who had the success of this procedure resting heavily on his shoulders.

As a living donor Bruno had to have routine checks to ensure he was suitable—health screening, physical exam, X-rays to check for signs of any kidney disease. His father also had to have pre-transplant tests to check for any signs of infection. The transplant couldn't go ahead if there was any problem with either the new organ or the patient.

Bruno's operation had already been completed, with the kidney safely removed, and by all accounts he was recovering well with no sign of infection or unusual blood loss. Although the kidney was able to survive out of the body for up to forty-eight hours, the optimal time from removal to transplant was four hours. A factor always on Seth's mind when the operation itself could take anywhere from ninety minutes to six hours depending on the complexity of the situation.

With the duke's bloods and urine tests satisfactory, Seth scrubbed into Theatre along with the anaesthetists and other attending medics. He'd carried out this operation countless times over the course of his career but there was even more pressure on him today to be the best at what he did. This was Kaja's father and the leader of an entire country.

Watching his progress on the monitor, Seth

made several small surgical cuts under Olov's ribs. Each one a reminder that he had the responsibility of this man's life in his hands.

This keyhole technique, while delicate, aided speed of recovery when there were smaller incisions to heal. While there was no need to remove the damaged organs, he would have to hitchhike the blood into the new kidney.

He wished he could apply a similar procedure to his relationship with Kaja so they could live with the damage from their past and use the good parts to jump-start a new working relationship. He couldn't continue banishing her from the hospital to avoid their personal issues. Once this surgery was over he needed to hold out an olive branch and hope she didn't use it to whip him.

Now he'd consigned himself to making reparations with Kaja, he focused on his patient, whose body was lying open to him.

'Clamp, please.'

He isolated the renal vein, and iliac artery and the new kidney was retrieved from cold storage ready to be transplanted.

It was a demanding, technical operation but there was satisfaction seeing the kidney turn pink and come back to life as it was warmed up with a warm saline solution.

Seth wondered if his relationship with Kaja could ever be resurrected in a similarly healthy fashion.

Once he was certain everything was working as it should, they began closing. Only then was he able to relax a bit, content he'd done his job to the best of his abilities. Equally important, he could tell Kaja the transplant had been a success.

'Miss Kaja! I don't know what to do. I know you are very busy with your poor brother and father...' Fatima crossed herself as she ran into Kaja's room.

'Fatima, what's wrong?' She didn't have the time or energy for any more dramatics. She was exhausted. Drained by the emotions and intensity of the day so far. Not only because of her worry about her family members but she was trying to fathom the reasons behind Seth's sudden personality change. He'd never spoken to her so abruptly before and she wasn't sure what she'd done to deserve it other than be concerned for her family's welfare. Whatever his reason, it was clear he'd wanted her out of the way.

Unfortunately, with all of that running through her mind she hadn't been able to shut her brain down even for a few hours' sleep. Despite Seth's insistence, being at home hadn't made her any less anxious.

'I had a phone call…my sister needs me. She's had a fall and been taken to hospital. I must go and see her but what about you and Miss Amy? I can't leave you alone.' Poor Fatima sounded as though she was about to have some sort of breakdown as she wrung her apron with her hands.

'Yes, you can. Take as much time as you need to look after your sister. Now, where's Amy?'

'She is sleeping. Are you so very sure you can manage without me?' Seeing Fatima's distressed face, Kaja was tempted to say no to assure her she was indispensable. She had managed alone for the longest time but Fatima was a comfort to her when she needed it. A mother figure providing some sense of belonging where she no longer felt she had any.

'We will do our best to cope while you are away. Don't worry about us. Go, be with your sister. Family must take priority.'

'Thank you.' Fatima kissed her on both cheeks and the gratitude expressed for a few days' leave humbled Kaja. She'd become so engrossed in her own world and problems she'd selfishly forgotten Fatima had a life outside the palace. The woman she took for granted was needed and loved by her own family too. It would do them both good to be reminded of that.

'Take as much time as you need and let us know how your sister is keeping.' Although it might have sounded like an afterthought she was genuinely concerned and decided taking an interest in Fatima's personal affairs was long overdue. It might stop some of this continuous self-pity she'd been indulging in for too long.

It was only when she waved her devoted companion off that Kaja realised what she'd agreed to. She was taking charge of Seth's daughter in Fatima's absence. Without his knowledge or permission.

Kaja couldn't relax. She couldn't focus on the book she was attempting to read, the words blurring every time she looked at the page as her mind wandered. There was too much going on for her to sit on her plush plum velvet banquette surrounded by plump cushions pretending she didn't have a care in the world.

Despite any appearance of her as a princess lounging around waiting for her prince to come and rescue her, her nerves were shredded to ribbons. She was on high alert, ears straining for the sound of the telephone call from the hospital, or a sign of Amy stirring in her bedroom. The afternoon was a fraught one as she waited for it to be disturbed. Even more so now she had to come up with some idea of how to entertain a four-year-old. She had little experience of children, save for those she'd treated in a medical capacity. It was important to get this right for Amy because if she was upset, Seth would be too. More so than he apparently already was with her.

Not only did she want to prevent Amy from becoming bored and starting to miss her father, but she had to prove to Seth she was capable of taking care of his daughter. If she let him down again he'd never forgive her.

Kaja didn't know how long she'd been sitting here in Seth's apartment waiting to be useful to someone. Every tick of the brass clock on the mantelpiece seemed longer and louder than ever, echoing around the empty lounge. With only Seth's personal effects for company.

His jacket, clearly redundant in these current temperatures, was slung over the back of a chair. A pair of trainers sat by the door ready for his early morning jog around the palace gardens. The one she watched from behind her bedroom curtain and which had steadily become the highlight of her days. There was a stack of crime thrillers sitting perilously on the side table by her seat and a trail of Amy's toys stretched across the carpeted floor. It already looked like a family home. Lived in. She was sure he'd dismissed any member of staff who'd offered to tidy and clean the rooms, regardless that he was too busy to do it himself.

These were signs of a man content with who he was, without a need to impress anyone else. She envied him that freedom along with that one huge responsibility who demanded his time and attention.

Kaja lifted one of Amy's pink plastic teacups from the floor. Father and daughter had obviously been having a tea party together before he'd gone out to do his other job as a life-saving surgeon. It was such a simple indulgence of his daughter but the image it conjured up brought a smile to her lips and a pang in her heart. That was the kind-hearted, warm man she remembered. Someone who'd never be too busy to play with his child because he understood the gift he'd been given. Not everyone was lucky enough to be a parent.

Seth might have appeared a distant stranger to her in comparison but there was one thing that continued to niggle her. If he remained resentful about their past relationship, or as indifferent to her as he'd have her believe, why on earth had he come here? He had plenty of work at home and clearly no desire to tread old ground on a romantic level so what had prompted him into helping her? Seth didn't owe her a thing. It was the other way around. She couldn't help but think that the only reason he had for coming out was the unfinished business between them.

A shiver of excitement tickled the back of her neck. He must have forgiven her to some extent to have considered her request to help her father. Perhaps his love for her hadn't simply died the way she'd believed after hearing about his subsequent nuptials. He'd practically told her he'd done that on the rebound.

Kaja tried her best not to get carried away by the idea. Given recent events, she had a long way to go to get him to even talk civilly to her again. Besides, even if their feelings for one another hadn't evaporated completely, their circumstances wouldn't be any more compatible now. They were still worlds apart and he had his daughter's feelings to consider along with his own. She stared into the plastic receptacle wishing it could tell her fortune, map out her future for her when she couldn't do it herself. As much as she had wanted Seth to look at her the way he used to, she was afraid awakening old feelings was a wasted exercise.

Kaja was plagued by the confusion over what it meant to have him back in her life. She still couldn't be the woman Seth needed her to be.

It was exhausting being in her head. When she heard Amy's little feet patter across the floor it was a relief to have something else to focus on.

'Hello, sleepyhead. Fatima had to go home to her family for a little while. Her sister's very poorly.'

The four-year-old was still rubbing her eyes when she wandered in, her clothes and hair in disarray. 'Like your daddy?'

Kaja's heart lurched, surprised that the child had picked up on what was going on in the adult world around her.

'Not quite, but she's in hospital and Fatima has gone to visit.'

Amy thought for a moment. 'Can Daddy fix her too?'

'Your daddy is very busy but Fatima's sister will have a doctor like him to take care of her.' That seemed to be enough to satisfy her curiosity as Amy climbed up onto the settee and tucked her legs beneath her.

'I'm hungry. Fatima said we were going to make cookies and play hide and seek.'

'I guess that's what we're doing, then. Let me get changed and I'll take you down to the kitchen.' That took care of how she was going to keep Amy occupied for the afternoon. Only time would tell if Seth would be appeased so easily on discovering Fatima's replacement.

CHAPTER FIVE

'LET ME KNOW when they're ready for visitors,' Seth instructed the staff in the intensive care unit before exiting the hospital.

At this moment he was regretting telling Kaja to send away her chauffeur and stretch limo. His job might not involve heavy manual labour but it was exhausting just the same. The intense concentration, knowing the fatal consequences if he messed up, along with the hours spent on his feet took their toll mentally and physically. He was sorry he didn't have someone to pick him up outside and deliver him to Kaja's door.

The short stroll he undertook suddenly became a marathon when his whole body was crying out for rest.

It wasn't only shunning a bit of luxury he was kicking himself for either. He'd been short with Kaja today. Not at all supportive at a time when she needed it because he was too wrapped up in his own issues. If he'd been dealing with the family of any other transplant patient he would've been more sympathetic. He hadn't been fair treating her differently at such an emotive time. If this had been either of his grandparents, or, heaven forbid, Amy, he would've been beside himself with worry too. Sending her away hadn't been his call to make.

He had no right to be rude to her simply because he was afraid of getting too close again. Behind all the glamour and privilege, he could see she was still the same woman he'd wanted to marry. The problem with that was she'd already rejected him once before. After a divorce, losing his gran and with all of the baggage his mother had left him with, those shutters around his heart should've been on lock down. Yet he kept thinking of the good times he and Kaja had once shared, scuppering any chance of remaining impervious to her charms.

Since Kaja wasn't party to the complicated web of thoughts causing him to act so unreasonably, he wanted to deliver the news about the surgery in person rather than let her hear it in a two-second phone call where he was desperate to get off the line. It was an effort of reparation on his part and would give her a chance to voice any question she might have. This wasn't about him and Kaja, it was about her and her family. That was why he was here. If she tore strips off him for the way he'd spoken to her today he'd have to stand and take it. It was the least he deserved in the circumstances.

'Seth Davenport.' He waved his ID at security as he'd become accustomed. Regardless that they knew him by sight now he had to wait until they waved him through and some unknown entity opened the gates.

As after every other tense shift, he was looking forward to some downtime with his daughter. He needed some normality more than ever. An uncomplicated period where nothing was asked of him other than loving his daughter. Something he didn't need to work at when she was the only person he could guarantee wouldn't want him out of her life.

'Hello?' His voice echoed around the hall, eliciting no response. It was so different from the usual homecoming he received when Amy launched herself at him, pleased to have him to herself again. Here, everything seemed flat, lifeless, lonely. It was impossible not to pity

Kaja if this was what she came back to on a regular basis.

Despite his weariness Seth jogged up the stairs to his apartments, eager to get to his daughter and that familiar sense of home, family and being loved.

There was no sign of Nils, which wasn't surprising since he'd told him in no uncertain terms he didn't need assistance. Fatima was a different story. Seth wouldn't have been able to work without her looking after Amy and the two had already forged a bond, which he took as confirmation his daughter was content. That was all that mattered.

He was surprised the two of them hadn't come haring straight at him the second he'd come through the door. Along with Amy's demand for his attention he'd become used to the older woman constantly trying to feed him up.

'I'm home!' The sound of an excited squeal reverberated around the entire floor of the building but his daughter remained elusive.

He frowned, a tad put out but also too tired to go child-hunting just yet. Instead, he gave into exhaustion, kicked off his shoes and sank into an armchair, which was surprisingly comfy for something that resembled a golden throne. It was something he suspected had been chosen only for the aesthetics. Amy was clearly enjoying herself wherever she was and as long as she was happy he could afford to close his eyes for a moment.

He was about to nod off when the sound of bare feet slapping on the tiled floor and a familiar voice called him back from oblivion.

'I didn't realise you were home.'

He opened his eyes to see Kaja skidding to a halt in front of him and was momentarily lost for words. Like his daughter standing beside her, Kaja's face was splattered with either mud or chocolate, or both. The elegant princess had been replaced with a ragamuffin. Her sleek, perfectly coiffured glossy hair had been tied up into a messy ponytail. Loose tendrils, which had escaped during her obvious exertions with his daughter, clung damply to her rosy cheeks. However, it was her choice of outfit that made him do a double take. She'd swapped the chic trouser suit he'd seen her in this morning for something more practical.

With one swipe she transferred most of the

chocolatey mud onto the sleeve of her—his—oversized grey sweatshirt.

'I think I recognise that.' He nodded towards the hoodie she'd teamed with a pair of loose tracksuit bottoms.

Kaja's cheeks pinked a little more. 'Um... yeah, I think this one's yours. It was the only comfy thing I could find. My wardrobe isn't exactly conducive to childminding.'

Seth could only imagine the carnage if her expensive silks had been plastered in the same way as his old university sweater. She looked like the old Kaja standing there wearing her favourite item of his clothes. He wondered if it had accidentally found its way into her suitcase when she'd fled or if she'd packed it as a reminder of him. His bruised ego and wounded heart hoped it was the latter and that she'd thought of him, might have even missed him over the years. As he had her.

He decided not to reference her clothing any further or attach any significance to it aloud. Not when she'd essentially told him she'd only worn it because it was dispensable and it didn't matter if it got dirty or torn.

'Why are you minding Amy? Where's Fatima?'

He didn't know if it was more surprising that the officious older woman had abandoned her post or that the previously stand-offish Kaja had enthusiastically stepped up in her place.

'Fatima had a family emergency. I'm afraid she's had to return home for a while. I hope you don't mind but I've been looking after Amy in her absence.'

'Not at all. Thank you. I hope everything's okay with Fatima.' How could he object to her stepping in when she was doing everyone a favour? It had simply come as a surprise to see Kaja like this, playing with his daughter and looking more carefree than he'd seen her since he arrived.

'On the subject of family...' Kaja was toying with the elasticated cuffs of her sweatshirt. Fidgeting was always an indicator of how anxious she was about something and there were no prizes for guessing what that was today. It wasn't fair to keep her in the dark any longer.

'Amy, why don't you go and wash your face while I have a talk with Kaja?'

'Will you play hide and seek with us after?'

'Sure. Now go. Shoo.' He clapped his hands and Amy scuttled off with a giggle.

'You sure have a way of getting people to do what you want.' Kaja's sardonic tone was to be expected after their last encounter.

'I'm sorry for the way I spoke to you earlier. I was out of line.'

'You think?' She folded her arms across her chest, fending off his attempt to apologise.

'It wasn't my place to tell you to leave the hospital but I promise I was doing it with the best of intentions. I didn't want to think of you sitting in the corridors all day fretting about something you had no power to control.' That was the main problem. He was worried he'd be distracted by thoughts of her so close by while he was busy saving her father's life.

She waved away his explanation with the hand she'd now untucked from her defensive position. 'All that aside, you didn't call. Does that mean something went wrong? Are Papa and Bruno okay?'

'Everything's fine. I just wanted to tell you in person. The transplant went as planned and they're both recovering now. Someone will page me when they're ready for visitors and we can go and see them together.' He waited for Kaja's exclamation of relief, braced himself for her enthused gratitude, certain she'd forgive him now, but she remained stock-still and wide-eyed.

'Kaja? Did you hear me? They're going to be all right.' He wished she would say something, even if it was to swear at him. Instead she'd gone into some sort of shock. Seth was contemplating shaking her out of her stupor when she suddenly burst into tears. Her whole body appeared to collapse into itself as she finally took in what he was saying. A tsunami of all that emotion she'd apparently been holding back.

'Oh, sweetheart.' Any resentment he might have subconsciously harboured over their break-up dissipated along with the notion that theirs should remain a strictly professional relationship when she was so clearly in need of a hug.

It was pure instinct that drove him to catch her in his arms and provide that comfort and support she must've been lacking to fall apart in front of him. She didn't rail against his compassion, instead, crumpling against him in emotional exhaustion. He dreaded to think what it would have done to her if she'd had bad news.

'Let it all out.' Seth held her close, his arms wrapped tightly around her to keep her upright and let her tears soak through his shirt. That protective need to take care of her hadn't left him. Even though these were tears of happiness he knew she needed someone to lean on who understood her. Someone who knew she hated showing any weakness and would hold her until it passed without thinking less of her. She needed him. That superseded his, probably futile, endeavours to emotionally detach himself from the only woman he'd ever truly loved.

'All clean, Daddy.' Amy burst in again reminding them that time and their relationship had moved on and comforting Kaja was no longer in his job description.

'Good girl.' He praised his daughter and ruffled her hair, giving Kaja time to wipe her eyes and take a step away from him.

'What's wrong with Kaja?' Quick to notice all wasn't well, Amy frowned at him as though he'd obviously done something to upset her. Seeing the thunderous look on her face, he had a hunch she'd take her new friend's side if she had to choose.

'I'm fine, honey. Your daddy just gave me

some really good news.' Kaja's eyes and smile shone a bit too brightly as she faced Amy, making Seth inclined to hug her a little longer.

'Is your daddy all better?' Amy's frown evened out into a smile and, though it would be easier to let her think everything was all rainbows and unicorns, he preferred to be honest with his daughter.

'We hope so. He needs to stay in hospital for a while to make sure.'

Amy digested that new information before asking her next question cautiously. 'Does that mean we can keep playing hide and seek?'

'I don't see why not.' Kaja pulled her into an embrace, making Seth proud of the child he'd raised who'd consider someone else's feelings before thinking of herself. Unlike her father this morning.

The squealing and running about that had woken him made more sense now. Hide and seek always made Amy excitable, though her hiding places required a high level of acting on his behalf to pretend he couldn't see her feet sticking out from beneath the curtains.

'Good. I'm it this time. You and Daddy go and hide.'

Seth and Kaja looked at each other with the same expression of horror before stumbling over each other's excuses to avoid being paired for the game. Regardless that he'd lent her his shoulder to cry on, there were several layers of unresolved tension between them, which weren't conducive to playing happily together.

'I'm sure your daddy needs a rest after working all day—'

'You and Kaja were having plenty of fun without me—'

Amy ignored their protests, putting her hands over her eyes as she began to count. 'One, two, three…'

His daughter had a habit of getting him into all kinds of predicaments but this one topped the lot. Playing hide and seek with an ex-girlfriend who probably despised him more now than when she'd dumped him wasn't awkward at all.

He looked at Kaja but she shrugged her shoulders, apparently unwilling to help him find a way out of this. When she took off running his competitive nature rose to the fore with his pride at stake if he couldn't outwit a four-year-old.

At the adorable sound of Amy trying to count, sometimes stumbling over her numbers, missing a few, and repeating others, he did his best to find a suitable hiding place. It wasn't easy at his size but Kaja hadn't had a problem since she'd disappeared completely from view.

He dived under his bed only to be met with a painful roadblock, forgetting he'd stashed his suitcase there.

'Ready or not, here I come!' Amy sing-songed with glee.

Crawling back out from his failed hiding place, Seth searched frantically around his room for a last-minute alternative. He yanked open the wardrobe door and jumped inside as Amy's footsteps echoed down the hall.

It was only when he closed the door it became apparent he wasn't alone. Before his eyes managed to adjust to the dark he heard the distinct sound of someone breathing next to him. He batted his way through the row of hanging shirts seeking the source.

'Kaja?' he whispered. 'I hope to goodness it's you in here and not some creepy stalker hiding in my closet.' It was disorienting in the cramped dark space. Not to mention unnerving knowing he wasn't alone.

'Do you get many of those?'

'You'd be surprised.' He didn't care that she was making fun of him if it took her mind off everything else that had gone on today.

'Where are you? It's disconcerting hearing a disembodied voice in the dark.'

'Tell me about it.'

He heard her shift position, then felt hands patting across his chest and up to cup his face. 'Ah, there you are.'

She inched closer until he could see the twinkle of her eyes shining in the shadows as she toyed with him. The soft touch of her hands on his skin made him temporarily forget to breathe. All he could do was stare at her beautiful smile and remember how it used to be to wake up next to it in the morning.

'Kaja… I really am sorry about the way I behaved at the hospital today. I didn't mean to upset you.' When they were here, so close to one another, it was impossible to maintain that detachment he'd been striving for. He wasn't fooling anyone, least of all himself.

'I was too full on, fussing around Bruno and

my father when you were just trying to get on with your work.'

He reached out and brushed his fingers along the side of her cheek. 'It wasn't your fault. This is on me.'

'Well, you've apologised, more than once, and held me while I cried like a baby.'

Seth saw the sheen of tears in her eyes again and he had no choice but to reach out to her so she knew she had some support. 'That's nothing to be ashamed of when you've been dealing with so much. I'm always available for hugs should you need them.'

'I'm going to hold you to that.' She sniffed as she leaned her head against his chest and wound her arms around his waist with a sigh.

His attempts at being emotionally closed off from Kaja were short-lived when her every tear was a hit to his solar plexus. He couldn't bear to see her hurting and when she was clinging on to him like this, trusting him to provide her with some comfort, he could almost forget they'd ever parted. A treacherous path to venture down with someone who'd almost destroyed him once before.

'Come out, come out, wherever you are...'

Amy's Child-Catcher-like song encouraged Kaja to giggle. A sweet, welcome sound in the aftermath of today's stresses.

When she looked up at him he placed a finger on her smiling lips. 'Shh!'

They locked eyes in the darkness, their bodies still entwined with only the sound of their synchronised breathing to be heard. Although, he was sure it had become more ragged over the course of the past few minutes. This wardrobe had suddenly become their whole world. Population two.

Kaja's mouth parted beneath his touch, her breath hot against his skin. He remembered the honeyed taste of those lips and the way they moulded perfectly to his even though it seemed so long ago now. Tentatively, he drew his finger down, slowly uncovering her delectable mouth. He wanted, needed to kiss her when she was looking up at him with equal longing, drawing him down towards her, encouraging him to act on his urge.

'Found you!' Bright light infiltrated their cosy cocoon once Amy discovered them, flinging both doors open wide. Kaja's arms fell away from the embrace, leaving him bereft. It had been so long since he'd felt that intimate inter-action it came as a shock to be reminded he wanted it. That beneath his roles as a father and a doctor he was simply a man with needs of his own. Her touch had reawakened feelings he'd put on hold in the pursuit of being the best parent he could be for his daughter. Only Kaja had the ability to do that.

Since she was an ex who'd rejected his mar-riage proposal and he was currently treating her family members, he knew exploring that route would only lead to trouble. Especially when they were living under the same roof and now sharing his daughter's care. Renewing their re-lationship would be a bad move for all manner of reasons, primarily that she'd already bro-ken his heart and he couldn't go through that again. Nor would he inflict that pain on his daughter when she was growing closer to Kaja by the minute. As far as Amy was concerned, once his patients had recovered they'd be fly-ing home. He wanted to keep it that way rather than let her think Kaja was going to be part of their lives only to have her run out when it all got too real.

Seth stepped out into the real world leaving

Kaja in the land of make believe where a kiss was possible and wouldn't cause a multitude of problems.

'You are too good, Amy Davenport. I think you deserve a prize for finding us so quickly. Why don't I take you out for a special treat?' He put his hand on his daughter's back and ushered her out of the door. Thankfully, she was so jubilant at having found them she hadn't picked up on the tension between the adults. He wished it were going to be so easy for him to put the incident out of his mind and dismiss what could have ended up as their second first kiss.

Kaja was tempted to close the closet doors and slink back into the shadows. Seth was making it clear he didn't want to spend any more time with her. He couldn't even look at her. She knew why. A moment together, unguarded and isolated from their responsibilities outside this room, and old feelings had been given space to breathe. Another second alone and she knew they would have given into temptation to kiss, to touch and taste one another again.

She'd been on her own for too long. Well, she'd been living with her family and the entourage of staff her father insisted upon, but she'd been short of actual company. Why else would she have turned to an ex in her hour of need? Clearly, she was confusing her gratitude for the surgeon who'd saved her father's life with desire.

She'd known from the start having Seth here was going to be difficult, but she'd thought putting her father's health above her failed romance should take precedence. That was until she'd become aware that the physical attraction between them hadn't lessened over the years. She'd wanted him to kiss her and if Amy hadn't busted them she was pretty sure he would have.

'Can Kaja come too?' Amy's plea for her to be included put a stop to any thoughts of slinking away unnoticed. It also prevented Seth from leaving the room as quickly as he'd intended.

Realising it would look strange if she continued to hide in the wardrobe, she had no choice but to step back out into the spotlight.

Gone was the passion burning in Seth's eyes for her, replaced with a look of frustration. He didn't want her hanging around with him and his daughter. Whatever that moment had been between them, it was over.

'I'm sure Kaja would rather wait here until the hospital rings with news.'

'I'm not really dressed for going out, Amy.'

'Right, and it would take ages to organise cars and security.' Seth was quick to add to the list of excuses why she couldn't go with them but they both knew the real reason he didn't want her tagging along. They'd almost kissed in there and he wanted to put some distance between them so they'd forget it had ever happened. It stung to have him reject her so casually when the moment had literally made her go weak at the knees. There hadn't been anyone since Benedikt. She hadn't even been tempted. Until now. Probably because she knew the passion of Seth's kisses, wanted them and was surprised he still looked at her with that same burning desire. After everything she'd done to him, she knew he would never hurt her and for a lonely divorcee that was the greatest aphrodisiac of all.

'We don't have to go out, Daddy. Me and Kaja made cookies. Can't I have some of those for my treat?'

Amy always had an answer for any obstacles preventing her from getting what she wanted.

It was a credit to Seth how smart she was, and determined. He'd raised a strong daughter and Kaja bet there was never a dull moment in the Davenport household.

'I...er...'

'I did promise Amy we could sample some once they'd cooled.' She watched with increasing amusement as Seth tried desperately to come up with another counter argument and failed. They were only going down to the kitchen to scoff a few biscuits. It wasn't as if they were on their own and about to act out some erotic scene from the contents of the fridge. Not unless he asked her to...

CHAPTER SIX

'THEN I SUPPOSE we have no choice...'

Amy was Seth's conscience as well as his get-out clause. He had tried to use her to run away from his resurging feelings for Kaja. He'd wanted to kiss her and he'd come close to it. When they'd been fooling around, the only thought in his head had been that need to be with her again. The time he'd spent worrying where she'd gone, what he'd done wrong and how he was going to live without her dismissed all too easily. Worrying when she had the power to make him feel as rejected and unwanted as his mother had by her absence in his life.

What he didn't understand more than his own reaction was why Kaja had been leaning in for that kiss in the first place. Not only because he'd been abrupt with her today, but she was the one who'd ended their relationship. While he might have unresolved emotions and issues, Kaja had made her feelings pretty clear five years ago. She didn't want him. What had changed in their time apart? Nothing as far as he knew. It was possible she was simply lonely out here and had been confused by his company and their romantic history.

He wasn't going to mistake his feelings towards Kaja for anything other than a want for her, which apparently hadn't died simply because she'd left him. More than that, left him open to be hurt all over again.

They were different people now but the problems that had taken Kaja away from him in the first place remained. He didn't belong as a permanent feature in her life any more than she did in his. She lived in a different country, moved in higher social circles, was born royal. Their backgrounds couldn't be more different or incompatible. Rejection had been an all too common feature in his life and he'd sworn not to put himself in a position to let it happen again. If this trip had been the ultimate test of that vow, he was failing miserably.

Thankfully, Amy's appearance snapped him back to his senses and made him willing to forget the incident ever happened and redouble his efforts to protect his battered heart. Except Kaja apparently had bewitched his daughter too, preventing total escape. There was no way he could forbid contact between them simply to prevent himself from making any further potentially disastrous decisions. It wouldn't be fair to either Amy or Kaja and would give them both cause to despise him.

Tensions were already running high around here without doing anything to upset either princess in his presence.

Despite his resolve to remain unmoved by his reacquaintance with Kaja, he was persuaded into the kitchen by two aspiring, giggling chefs to taste their goods.

'What about this one?' Amy, sitting on a high stool, was force-feeding him the misshapen biscuits she'd made. The crunchy brown lumps weren't appetising in either appearance or taste but she was so proud of them he couldn't refuse.

'Delicious,' he managed to utter through a mouthful of crumbs.

'I thought you preferred these?' Kaja popped

a delicate shell-shaped cookie into his mouth with a mischievous grin.

'No, he likes mine better.' A laughing Amy wedged another lump into his full mouth and Seth realised he'd become the butt of their joke. They weren't competing for his praise, they'd joined forces until his cheeks were bulging like a hamster storing sunflower seeds, and he was in danger of going into a sugar coma.

It had just been the two of them as a family for so long it was a new experience to have someone else join their fun. Paula had never been part of Amy's life so the only mother figure she'd known was his gran and he doubted she remembered much of that time, being so little. Watching her with Kaja was a bittersweet experience. In different circumstances perhaps this could have been a real family scene between them. Something he'd always wanted and, judging by the delight on his daughter's face, something she would like too.

He was a good father but that couldn't make up for the lack of a mother in her life. Someone she could confide secrets to that she didn't want to share with her father and someone to gang up with and play pranks on him. He'd pictured this life with Kaja. It was a shame she hadn't wanted it. She'd given up their future to return to her duties as a princess. He hadn't been enough incentive for her to stay when she'd made her choice five years ago. That was something he'd do well to remember instead of believing it could still be possible.

'Stop! I'll be sick if I eat any more, you rascal.' He tickled Amy, incapacitating her with laughter so she couldn't do any more damage to his waistline.

'Nonsense. I know you, Seth. I'm sure you haven't eaten anything all day.' Kaja dipped one of her golden-brown morsels into a bowl of melted chocolate sitting on the worktop.

She knew him too well. With a day of surgery ahead of him he hadn't stopped to refuel since the breakfast Fatima had provided this morning.

Kaja made sure hunger raised its head again as she bit down, the chocolate coating her lips, keeping Seth mesmerised as she licked it off with her pink tongue. Somehow, he'd turned another playful moment into an erotic display in his lustful mind. It didn't help matters when she dipped another cookie into the chocolate and offered it to him. He couldn't resist, even though he knew it was bad for him.

The confection was sweet on his tongue but nothing compared to the taste of Kaja as he sucked the remaining chocolate from her fingers. His eyes didn't leave hers, watching until they darkened and a small gasp sounded from her lips.

'Where's my chocolate?' Once again Amy saved him from himself, demanding to be included in this new game.

'Last one before dinner.' He half coated another and gave it to the appreciative audience before washing away the chocolate on his fingers at the sink. Anything to get away from temptation and a woman with whom he seemed determined to tread old ground.

'I'll put the rest away for later.' At the other end of the kitchen Kaja busied herself parcelling up the remainder of the treats, but he could see her sneaking glimpses at him when she thought he wasn't looking.

This push and pull between them was torture. Especially when he already knew how good they were together on a physical level. It was geography, class divide and a lack of honesty that had been their downfall. If her reason for leaving him had been not loving him, or that they'd no longer been attracted to one another, living under the same roof wouldn't have caused the same intense level of tension simmering between them. It might have been better for his peace of mind if she'd stayed mad at him.

'Your Highness, I'm so sorry I was gone for so long. Please forgive me.'

'Fatima?'

Kaja's faithful aide bustled into the kitchen as if from nowhere. She untied the headscarf keeping her curly brown hair in place and struggled out of her heavy coat, which made Seth sweat simply looking at it. He supposed she was accustomed to the climate but, as a visitor more used to inclement British weather, he found the temperature and humidity stifling.

Kaja seemed more stunned by her arrival than her outdoor wear. 'I wasn't expecting you back so soon. How is your sister?'

'She hurt her back but it's nothing serious. I telephoned her daughter and she's driving over to be with her. Now, let me get back to work and clean up this mess you've left in my kitchen.' After hanging up her coat she pulled a floral apron from a drawer and tied it around her waist, then herded them out of her territory.

Seth's phone vibrated in his pocket with a text message.

'That's the hospital. You can go and see your dad and Bruno whenever you're ready.' He halted their procession down the hallway to tell her immediately. Now there was no doubt about where, or with whom, he'd be spending the rest of the day.

Kaja dithered when he'd half expected her to race off at once. 'I need to change but, er, would you come with me?'

'To get changed?' She made it too easy for him to tease her but joking around was safer ground than those hot, loaded looks they kept exchanging.

She rolled her eyes. 'To the hospital.'

'Can I stay with Fatima?' Amy had already turned on her heel and was running back towards the kitchen before he could answer. Clearly, she hadn't been spoiled enough today. He couldn't begrudge her some attention from an alternative female role model than an ex they were both growing dangerously close to, however.

'Yes, Kaja, I'll accompany you to the hospital. I have to check on my patients anyway. Yes, Amy, you can stay with Fatima, if that's all right with her.' Seth addressed each of them in turn telling himself it was the right thing to do for all concerned.

'Okay, I'm ready to go. Sorry for the wait.' While Kaja wanted to sprint immediately to the hospital to see for herself that her family was safe, it wasn't as simple as that.

'No problem.' Seth rose from the armchair he'd been sitting in waiting for her to make herself presentable for the outside world.

It was easy for him. A quick shower and a change of shirt and he was ready. As handsome as ever. She needed a bit more assistance to be camera-ready in case she was snapped on the way. The chances of that happening were high with the press camped outside the front of the hospital waiting for news.

Her car was out front, engine running. Seth graciously helped her into the back seat before climbing in next to her. The photographers were there at the gates too, wanting to catch her reaction, some sign of what had happened to her father during surgery. It was draining having to keep up a façade when any display of emotion was deemed unbecoming for a member of the royal family. That was why she'd wanted Seth to accompany her. At least when she was with him she no longer had to keep that stiff upper lip. She'd already broken down in front of him, clung to him for support, and the world hadn't ended because she'd let someone in. Although it still could if she got too used to having him around.

'Thank goodness for tinted windows. They give some illusion of privacy even if the press always manage to sneak a picture somewhere along the way.'

'Don't you get sick of all this? Wish you could just run away from it all and live a normal life?' There was pity in Seth's eyes and she found it worse than the pain she'd seen there most of the time when he'd looked at her.

She didn't really deserve anyone's sympathy when she led such a privileged life. Regardless that she found it trying at times. People had been hurt worse than her in her pursuit of normality. Seth for one.

'I tried that, remember? I made my escape to England but running away doesn't solve problems. Everything catches up with you in the end. I'll never regret our time together, Seth, but I was living a lie. I'm sorry you got caught in the crossfire while I figured that out.' Her love for Seth had been genuine but coming back here only proved it could never have worked out. Protocol impinged on basic things most people took for granted, such as privacy. Something she knew Seth was struggling with in his short stay here so far.

Neither of them would want that kind of intrusion for Amy either. Playing together today, having fun like any other normal family, only served to increase her sense of loss. Being a mother was never going to be possible for her. The more time she spent with Amy, the more she realised what she was missing out on. Despite appearances, Seth was the one who had everything.

Perhaps she should've stayed single rather than ever getting involved with anyone. Then no one would have been hurt. Including her.

'I wish you'd told me that before I flew all the way out here.' There was that sad smile again, which wouldn't have been noticeable to someone who didn't know him as well as she did.

'Why?' There had been a couple of unguarded moments between them but Seth had been quick to stamp out any flames when heat sparked between them. She doubted rekindling their romance was the reason he'd agreed to help her father in the first place.

He sighed and leaned back into the leather. 'I think that's what I was doing by accepting your request to treat your father. After Gran died I was lost. Coming here has been a distraction from the reality of her no longer being around. If what you're saying is true, the grief will be waiting for me on my return.'

She fought back the sudden and surprising disappointment as he confirmed his motive had nothing to do with her and reached out to squeeze his hand. Seth glanced down at the fingers clasped around his, then up at her, his eyes misted with unshed tears.

There were similarities that had brought them to where they were now. She was apparently mourning their relationship and her chance to be mother to someone as wonderful as Amy as much as he was grieving the loss of his grandmother.

'It's not easy facing up to the things that keep you awake at night. I don't know how many times I rehearsed that call, dialled your number and hung up before I asked you for help. I know it's not the same but you'll feel better when you deal with your fears once and for all.' She'd thought of Seth often over the years, wanting to make amends but convincing herself to shove it all to the back of her mind and pretend to move on. When, in truth, she'd never got over him. Her heart hadn't let go of him simply because she'd thought it the right thing to do.

'Did it work? Do you think you've exorcised some demons by seeing me again?' He was searching her face for answers, making it difficult for her to lie to him.

Her blush would give her away anyway. She had no business dishing out advice when her life had been such a car crash up until now. Plus, if she was going to be honest with him it meant confessing she still had feelings for him. News that might not be welcome after everything she'd done.

'I'm glad I called. For my father's sake and I, um, I'm pleased I got to see you again. It gave me the chance to explain why I did what I did.'

'But… I get the sense this hasn't played out the way you imagined?' He was able to read her way too easily. Perhaps after being burnt so badly already he watched her more carefully these days.

She glanced out of the window trying to get her bearings. Why did this journey seem to take longer when she was in the car with him?

'I, uh…' she cleared her throat '… I didn't expect that we'd, uh, still have that spark.' Or that she'd be faced with the reality of her infertility issues again. Babysitting Amy reminded her what she was missing out on and even if circumstances made a relationship possible with Seth, she couldn't give him everything that should come with that.

The ensuing silence was interminable as she waited for him to confirm or deny her observation.

Then Seth said quietly, 'Nor me.'

There wasn't time to analyse what that meant for them other than it hadn't been all in her head as the car pulled up outside the hospital.

'Before we go in, I need you to be prepared. Remember, they've just come out of surgery. You know they're going to be weak and groggy.'

She nodded, not concerned about anything behind those doors other than seeing her family again. Despite her fears her father might not get through this, she'd always had faith in Seth's abilities. There was a long way to go until they could say her father was in good health but at least the transplant had gone to plan so far.

'I'm here for you,' he said, resting his hand gently on her arm.

She bit her lip to stop from begging him to hold her again as he'd done earlier. That connection with someone who expected nothing from her in return was invaluable. Something she hadn't appreciated as much as she should have when she'd had it.

Then there was that rush of arousal he still managed to incite with a mere look. Her heart, and body, were crying out for his touch but they couldn't do anything in public without causing an uproar.

Instead, they exited the car separately, ignoring the cameras and the microphones being thrust in their direction as security hurried them inside.

'Oh, Papa.' Kaja rushed to her father's bedside battling for space amongst the attachments and machines assisting his recovery. He had drips going into his body, drains coming out and a morphine driver for pain relief, but he was here.

'Kaja…my daughter,' he rasped through dry, cracked lips under his oxygen mask. The effort of opening his eyes to look at her proved too much and they fluttered shut again. He was obviously still tired. She'd never seen him so frail. He'd refused to let them accompany him when he'd been having dialysis and had always put on a brave face afterwards, even though he'd spent the rest of those days in bed. One to always defy his age and keep himself busy with the running of the country, now he was in his hospital gown without his tailored suits there was no hiding the truth. He was as vulnerable and mortal as everyone else.

His paper-thin skin was almost translucent, except for the lurid red and purple marks where his body had been through the wars. It was clear there would be a long recovery period.

Seth, who'd been talking to the other doctors about his meds to prevent rejection of the new organ, came over when she kissed her father's forehead.

'We should let you get some sleep, sir. I hate to drag you away again so soon but he needs as much rest as possible, Kaja.'

'I know. I just wanted to see him for myself. Can I look in on Bruno quickly too?'

'Sure. He's still next door.'

'I'll come back and see you again tomorrow, Papa,' she whispered before following Seth into the adjoining room.

'Hello, sis!'

'Bruno!' Seeing him sitting up in bed looking so well considering what he'd been through, she wanted to hug him so tightly. She saw the fleeting panic cross his face as she ran to him and reined herself in before she caused him any further pain.

'How are you feeling?' She settled for giving him a peck on the cheek instead.

'Sore,' he said with a grimace. 'How's Dad?'

Seth stepped forwards then to put his mind at ease. 'Everything went to plan. He's understandably tired but doing well.'

'He's awake?'

'Only briefly. He knew I was there at least.' Kaja would've hated for him to have woken up and found himself alone in a strange room.

'That's good. Maybe I'll get to see him to-morrow when I'm back on my feet?' Bruno looked hopefully at Seth to authorise the visit.

'We'll see how you both do overnight.' Seth apparently wasn't going to be swayed by sym-pathy when it came to his patients' recovery times. He was the kind of doctor who'd do whatever he could to buoy his patients' spir-its. It went a long way to aiding recovery. She'd seen for herself how much having beloved fam-ily members around helped people get better quicker compared to those left languishing alone with no visitors to boost their mood.

'Is there anything I can bring you from home, Bruno?' She wanted to do something, anything, to make her brother more comfortable when he'd sacrificed so much to save their father. The fact she hadn't been a match had put paid to any idea of her being a donor even if either of them would've let her do it. As a result, her conscience insisted she needed to pay some sort of penance because she wasn't the one lying in a hospital bed recovering from an operation.

He shook his head. 'I think I'm all set. I have books, magazines, puzzles and a phone somewhere.'

'Has Missy been in?'

'Where do you think I got the supplies from? I'm sure she'll be back later. I asked the staff to let her know when I was awake too.'

'In that case, I'll let you recharge your batteries. You've got to look your best for your sweetheart.' Her brother was still head over heels about his long-term girlfriend and vice versa. They made an adorable couple but she couldn't help but envy them their future together.

'Thanks for calling in, Kaja. Hopefully, next time I see you I'll be on my feet.' He flicked another glance at Seth.

'We'll see.' Her visiting companion refused to be drawn any further on the subject despite Bruno's plea. She knew her brother well enough to predict him ignoring all medical advice to try and get on his feet before he was ready. When they were out of earshot, where she couldn't be accused of being a tattle-tale, she'd tell Seth to keep an eye on him for that very reason.

'Get some sleep. I just wanted to call in and say hello.' She kissed her brother on the cheek for a second time, content to leave now she'd been assured he was his back to his mischievous self.

'In that case, hello and goodbye. I'll see you tomorrow and don't forget to bring my running shoes with you,' he teased one last time before lying back down and closing his eyes.

'He seems in good spirits.' Seth echoed her thoughts aloud as he closed the door behind them.

'It would appear so. Although my brother wouldn't be inclined to tell me if he was in any pain.' She couldn't resist another peek through the window, finding him already fast asleep.

'All the reports so far are positive so I don't think there's any real cause to worry.'

'Not that that will stop me,' she said with a self-deprecating grin.

'It must be nice having a sibling. Even if it is one more person to fret over on a daily basis.'

'We weren't always this close but, yes, I'd be lost without him now. Do you think you've missed out on something by being an only child?' Bruno had been another casualty of her selfishness during those years she'd spent incommunicado in England but he hadn't held a grudge. He'd welcomed her back with open arms and told her how much he'd missed his little sister. Kaja hated herself for the estrangement but it was in her brother's good nature to forgive and forget. She had a much harder job forgiving herself.

Perhaps if she'd been honest with Seth, he and Bruno would have been friends from the start.

'I was never lonely when Gran and Gramps were alive but now... It would be nice to have someone to lean on. You know, someone who understands what I'm going through.' He let out a sigh and Kaja knew how truly lucky she was to have the family she did. At least when her mother had passed away she hadn't grieved alone. Her father and brother had lifted her up when she'd been at her lowest. Seth had no one except his young daughter.

'I know it's not the same but you can talk to me, if it helps?'

'Thanks, but, um, this is only short term, remember?'

How could she forget when he was always so desperate to get away from her?

'I know Amy's a comfort to you but you know where I am if you need a listening ear.'

'She is, but it's made me realise I want more for her. Given the chance I'd like to settle down with someone again and give her a stable family life. Perhaps even give her a brother and sister. Although, I suppose you need a partner before there's any chance of that happening.'

Kaja faked a laugh to accompany his, ignoring the lead weight that had dropped into the pit of her stomach. The family he wanted wasn't something he'd find with her. A quiet, ordinary life was something she'd sacrificed long ago because it had never truly been her destiny. Seth, on the other hand, could still have it all. Without her.

'Where is my driver?' she demanded from the nearest security officer, the effort of hiding her heartache becoming too much to sustain on top of an already emotional day.

'I'll check for you now, ma'am.' The burly shadow clone began issuing orders over his walkie-talkie.

'Are you in a hurry to get back?'

She momentarily stopped pacing the corridor like a caged animal.

'Yes. No. Well, there's no point in hanging around here getting in the way.' As she was wont to do when reminded of her inadequacies, she wanted to lock herself away from the outside world and hold herself a pity party.

'I think Amy and Fatima were expecting a bit more time together. We could do with a time-out too. Between the stress of the op and, I'm sorry to say this, but the oppressiveness of that house, I think we need a break.'

'What are you suggesting? I'm all for a change of scenery but you know I have to run it past a lot of other people first.' He'd intrigued her but protocol spoiled any notion of spontaneity.

'That's my point. You need some breathing space and a distraction from all this stress. It's not good for your mental health to be cooped up all the time like a trapped bird. You need to spread your wings once in a while. Come on, while he's not looking. Let's bust out of this joint.'

Kaja glanced at the guard walking down the corridor in the opposite direction with his back to them, then at Seth's hand, which was wrapped around hers.

'I can't just disappear. All hell would break loose. They'll think I've been kidnapped, for goodness' sake.' She resisted as he tried to pull her away.

Seth narrowed his eyes and she could almost see his brain working overtime to come up with a solution. Then he turned back towards the door to Bruno's room. 'This should do the trick.'

He lifted the marker pen tied to the whiteboard, where someone had scribbled *Bruno Alderisi—No Food*, and added his own message in bold letters.

Taking a mental health day on doctor's orders. No need to look for us. Back soon.

He handed her the pen. 'Well, they're not going to take my word for it.'

She let out a titter in disbelief he was serious about this. They weren't merely ditching class like a couple of naughty schoolkids, he was asking her to go against all the rules in place to keep her safe.

'You're a grown woman and one who has

worried herself sick all day. Surely, an afternoon off isn't too much to ask for?'

It wasn't, unless you were part of a royal family being constantly scrutinised under a microscope. She thought about what Seth was offering, what he represented. A freedom she hadn't had since she'd left England, and him.

She took the pen off him, ignoring his triumphant grin, and signed her name to their sick note.

'I guess not. What's the worst that could happen?'

CHAPTER SEVEN

'WHAT ARE WE waiting for, then?' Seth tugged her by the hand again and this time Kaja let herself be led astray.

This naughty side of Seth's made him appear years younger than the serious surgeon dealing with her brother only moments ago. It was impossible for her not to get caught up in the moment. For a little while at least it would be nice to pretend they were the two young, carefree people they used to be. Except it wasn't as straightforward as giving her security the slip.

'Wait. I'm going to be recognised the second I set foot outside. We're not going to get very far with me looking like this.' She could hide her jewellery in her pocket and tie up her hair but the expensive, brightly coloured clothes were going to draw attention.

'We'll figure something out. For now we need to put some distance between us and your human shield there.'

Kaja chuckled as they hurried down the corridor hoping their escapade wouldn't be suddenly cut short or that they would cause too many problems for the staff. She simply wanted to have some fun for a change.

'This reminds of that time on night shift together. Remember?'

'How could I forget?' The husky tone of Seth's voice and the memory itself warmed Kaja from the inside out.

She didn't know why she'd chosen that particular intimate snapshot from their history together to share when it was a million miles away from who and where they were today. Even in her thin layers of silk she was burning up thanks to the images she'd conjured up in her head.

That night had been during their first flush of love when they'd wanted to spend every second together. Preferably in bed. Work and conflicting schedules had made it difficult to get that quality time. So, when they'd found themselves working together on an unusually quiet night shift they'd made the most of it.

'In here, quick!' He opened a door halfway down the corridor and pulled her inside.

'What are you doing? I didn't mean for us to recreate that night together. I have to be more discreet about these things now, Seth,' she spluttered as he shut them into the tiny store room.

He tried to stifle a laugh, then reached out and cupped her face in his hands. Kaja held her breath, convinced he was about to kiss her. The adrenaline spiking through her body indicated how much she wanted him to.

'As much as I would love to, that's not why I came in here. I thought you might want to get changed.' He directed her gaze to the rows of freshly laundered scrubs hanging on the rails above them. She'd been so concentrated on Seth and the thought of his mouth on hers she hadn't noticed their surroundings.

'Oh. Yes. Of course.' She turned away, breaking physical contact so he couldn't see her turn scarlet with mortification. Now he knew exactly where her thoughts had gone to he might change his mind about spending the rest of the day with her.

'I'll grab one of the lab coats.'

With her back still to him Kaja lifted down a plastic-wrapped set of scrubs, swearing to launder and return them as soon as possible. She slipped out of her purple jumpsuit and shimmied into the less flattering, baggy outfit. The thin gold rope belted around the waist of her discarded clothes doubled up as a makeshift hair tie as she caught her tresses up in a ponytail and she used a fresh towel to wipe away her make-up. Now she was no one remarkable at all. If only she could disguise her true self from Seth too, she might be able to stay out of trouble.

Seth slipped his arms into the sleeves of the crisp white coat despite the sweat already clinging to his back. He was all too aware of Kaja standing behind him stripped to her underwear. It had been a spur-of-the-moment decision to duck in here when she'd been looking for excuses not to take some time off. As had the notion of running away in the first place.

He wanted to make up for his behaviour this morning along with easing some of the sadness Kaja had been cloaked in since the day he arrived. Five years was a long time to hold a grudge when he had a successful career and a daughter he doted on. She was the one in pain now, a wild exotic bird trapped in a gilded cage here, and he wanted to do something to set her free again.

It had come at a cost. The reminder of their passionate encounter on that nightshift was something he couldn't get out of his head. Especially now she was so close, half naked, with her familiar perfume filling the air.

The sensual memory of the last time they'd been locked in a storage room, clothes in disarray, getting hot and heavy up against the wall, blazed brightly in his head. Even though they'd tried to be quiet Kaja had made those little moans that drove him crazy.

Damn, they had to get out of here fast.

'I'm ready when you are.' Kaja's quick change came not a moment too soon.

'Great. Once I'm sure we're all clear out there we'll head for the fire exit.' Seth's relief was short-lived when he spun round only for her disguise to steal his breath away. The fresh-faced, beautiful surgeon he'd fallen in love with at work was standing right before him.

'I'm not sure these go with the outfit but beggars can't be choosers.' She lifted her trouser leg to show off the purple, open-toed sparkly heels she was wearing.

Seth reminded himself he wasn't a Regency hero who should be bowled over by a well-turned ankle. 'As long as you can walk in them I think we should be fine.'

They were going to have to stop cosying up in tight spaces if he was to resist temptation for the duration of his stay. The way Kaja continued to look at him with that reflected longing was severely testing his restraint and rendering his broken heart a distant memory.

He cracked the door open a fraction and peered out. 'Corridor's clear. Let's go.'

Kaja followed him out and the few staff they passed didn't bat an eyelid.

'So far, so good,' she whispered with a hint of excitement in her voice. She really had been locked away in her princess tower for too long.

'Don't speak too soon.' He grabbed hold of her and pretended to study the chart pinned to the wall as another guard charged past them.

His heart was thumping so hard he swore their pursuer would hear it. It was crazy to have suggested this. More so to have acted upon it. Kaja was royalty and for all these guys knew he could've abducted her. If he wasn't careful he'd find himself locked up for kidnapping their precious princess. She was no longer a mere work colleague he could blow off some steam with when the mood struck.

It was only the sound of heavy work boots continuing on past that let him breathe again and stop him imagining the rest of his days doing hard labour.

'It's amazing what a change of clothes and a make-under can do,' Kaja tutted.

'Indeed.' He withdrew his arm from around her shoulder, aware he'd broken all sorts of etiquette today. Both royal and personal. However, he had more serious matters to deal with. If he wasn't careful he'd find himself taken out by a SWAT team.

Moving swiftly away from the commotion building elsewhere, Seth led her towards a side exit next to the ambulance bay. Heads down, they walked past the paramedics unloading a gentleman in a wheelchair, doing their best not to raise suspicion.

'Where are we going? Kaja was tottering along in her spiked heels struggling to keep up as they tried to get as far from here as quickly as possible.

'I have no idea. The only parts of this country I've seen are the airport and the palace. Both of which I'm guessing will be on lockdown by now.'

'This is your great plan? To bust me out of the hospital and what? Take me on a day trip around the car park? I'd have been better off at home.' It was no wonder Kaja was ticked off at him. He really hadn't thought this through. This level of risk should've had a reward at the end to be worth all the trouble. If he'd planned this properly there would've been chilled champagne and a gourmet picnic waiting for them on a secluded beach somewhere. He wasn't good at spontaneity when the unknown presented a threat to his well-being.

'Hey. It was a spur-of-the-moment decision. Give me some credit for trying to shake things up around here.'

'In case you missed it, we've had enough drama recently to last a lifetime.' She hopped along on one foot while trying to dislodge her shoe from the other. Once completely barefoot she stomped silently towards the patch of grass at the back of the car park.

'Look, we've managed to get some time away from rent-a-hunk. We can spend it discussing my inadequacies as a member of the resistance or we can make the most of it.' He cocked his head to one side and fluttered his dark eyelashes.

It had been a long time since he'd had to employ that move to win her over but he was pleased to see it had the same desired effect as she failed to hide her grin.

'Okay, okay. I'm glad you took the initiative. I've forgotten what it was like to play hooky every now and again. You're a bad influence, Mr Davenport.' The faux scolding only confirmed the decision had been the right one. For both of them. How long had it been since he'd had a break from being Mr Responsible too? They needed to cut loose for a while. If only to remember the people they used to be before life got in the way.

'Now we've established this is entirely my fault if anyone asks, perhaps you'd like to have some input? This is your country after all. I would've thought you'd have some idea where to hide out for a couple of hours?' Back in England they could've disappeared easily with open fields, forests or seaside towns a mere train stop away. He knew nothing about the hiding potential here and with their history they needed somewhere with plenty of space around them.

Kaja knew she was taking out her bad mood on the wrong person. It was herself she was mad at for agreeing to this when after a couple of minutes alone in a locked room she was back to having lustful thoughts about Seth. Now, to all intents and purposes, they were on the run. As if they needed this romanticised any more when he was the man who believed he was giving her some freedom back.

In a way he was, when every moment she spent with him made her feel like the Kaja who'd spent those years in England living a normal life.

Something she shouldn't be reliving when she was doing her best to live up to her family name.

'There is a place not too far from here where Bruno and I used to sneak off to when we were kids.' It was her time to take the lead, carefully

picking her way barefoot down the grassy in-
cline away from civilisation.

'Won't Bruno rat us out? Surely that'll be the
first place he'll think of if he hears you've gone
AWOL?' The more cautious Seth began to re-
emerge as he jogged down the slope to join her.
His fancy, dress shoes weren't coping on the
wet grass any better than her bare feet. Despite
today's warm weather it must've rained some
time during the night, ensuring Seth's every
other step was more of a slide. Adding even
more of an element of danger to their outing
when there was the extra risk of him falling
onto his backside at any given moment.

'First off, Bruno is probably asleep and the
chances are no one is going to wake him up
after donating a kidney to tell him his kid sister
has gone for a walk. Secondly, he'll have forgotten about this place by now. If it even exists
any more. Besides, he knows how exhausting
this whole royalty deal is, better than anyone.
Who do you think found this place and planned
our escape days in the old days?' Before Seth,
her brother was the only person who'd understood her need to get away. That was before
duty had called him away from their childhood

games and she'd realised the reality of the responsibilities of royal life when he'd no longer had time for her or anything else.

The unmistakable squeak of smooth leather losing its grip on wet grass sounded nearby, followed by muffled curses.

'Take your shoes off, Seth. Your socks too. There's something very liberating and earthy about being barefoot in the countryside.'

He leaned against a nearby tree to do as she'd suggested and rolled up the bottoms of his trousers so they didn't get wet.

'If this is what getting back to nature feels like, it's slimier than I imagined.' Any Austen-esque notions about romantic walks in the country were obliterated thanks to Seth's unpoetic observations.

'Man up. For someone who spends his days elbows deep in other people's innards you shouldn't be this squeamish.'

'I tend not to walk barefoot through the operating theatre,' he said with a heavy dose of sarcasm. 'So, where does this slimy green road lead to anyway? A technicolour world with flying monkeys and grass-resistant ruby slippers for all?'

'Tobel. It's a derelict medieval village. If there's anything left of it by now. It's far enough from the usual tourist routes to hopefully avoid detection.' To be honest she'd forgotten all about the place until now. It had been relegated to the back of her mind as merely a childhood fantasy. A mythical land she'd imagined exploring in the mists of time.

Now, treading familiar ground, there was a bloom of excitement coming to life at the prospect of seeing the place again and reliving those carefree days.

'Forgive me but it doesn't sound like the ultimate escape. What's the fascination with some old ruins and how far away are they?'

'It was a place for us to hang out without being studied like lab rats. We just played hide and seek, had a moan to each other about how unfair life was, drew chalk pictures on the walls... You know, the usual kid stuff.'

'You're breaking my heart here, Princess. Some of us only had a back yard to play in. Not a whole abandoned village.'

She stuck her tongue out and teased him right back. 'I know, I know, and all you had to play with was a stick and a hoop...'

'You cheeky—'

For a second she thought she might have actually offended him as he halted their woodland walk. When he started after her, tossing his shoes aside, she let out a squeal before taking off at high speed. It was exhilarating running through the forest, branches whipping past, her heels discarded in her desire to escape Seth's false indignation. His deep laugh was sweeter than the sounds of the chirping birds watching them from high up in the treetops and she began to wonder why she was running at all.

Fate stepped in and plonked an exposed tree root in her path, causing her to trip.

'Are you okay?' Seth caught up with her in time to see the inelegant display as she landed face down on the ground.

She rolled over and sat up, dusting the dirt and leaves from her hands. 'I'm fine. It's only my pride that's taken a knock.'

'Let me give you a hand up and I swear I'll say nothing about karma.' He held out his hand to help her back onto her feet but the smug grin on his face demanded payback.

She slapped her palm against his but instead of letting him pull her up, she yanked his hand, unbalancing him so he too fell victim to the trip hazard.

Seth stumbled over the root and landed on top of her.

'S-sorry. Clearly I don't know my own strength.' She swallowed as his chest pressed so hard against hers she could feel his every rapid breath. His hands were either side of her head, braced on the ground giving him every opportunity to lever himself off her if he chose to. He didn't.

Instead, he dipped his head lower, his eyes not leaving hers, waiting for her to stop him. She couldn't find the words, or the inclination, to do so. He hesitated for a heartbeat, lips hovering so close to hers she could almost taste him. That need to kiss him suddenly consumed her body and soul. The soft pressure of his mouth on hers immediately gave way to something more passionate, more intense, more than a mere kiss.

Kaja closed her eyes and surrendered to the thrill of having Seth all to herself again. She wound her hands in his hair, revelling in the silky curls beneath her fingers, pulling him towards her to deepen their connection. Mouths and tongues entangled, breath hot and ragged, it was clear they'd both giving up fighting this powerful attraction defying their separation. For once, she didn't think about anyone else. Seth was everything. They could've been locked back in that stock room on the night shift again or tangled up in the sheets of their old double bed when the need for one another was just as great.

She shifted position, parting her thighs so Seth's body was hard against her right where she needed him most. He groaned.

'Kaja…what are you doing to me?'

The second he spoke she knew the spell had been broken.

He stopped kissing her and pulled away. She lifted her head and tried to coax him back into that blissful abyss of blood-rushing lust with kiss after kiss. Pride and dignity took a back seat in her desire to fall back into that fantasy world where only the two of them existed. Seth's touch made her forget everything bad in her life to focus on the way he made her feel. Damn good.

'We can't do this.' This time he did push himself up off her, leaving her hands empty and her body cold.

'It was only a kiss,' she said, trying to claw back some dignity as she hugged her knees to her chest to find some comfort. Aware she had been the one trying to turn it into something more.

He fixed her with his heavy-lidded eyes and gave a coy half-smile. 'Kaja, you know with us it's never going to be only a kiss.'

Seth didn't appear ashamed of succumbing to his desire, only afraid of where it would lead. Kaja understood that fear when it was exactly the same reason she should be resisting. Their circumstances might be different now but they still faced the same obstacles. Only now with added complications.

Less defensive now she knew it wasn't her he was rejecting, but the implications if they took things any further, Kaja got back on her feet. It was only then she realised she'd hurt her ankle as it buckled under her.

'Ow!' She grabbed for Seth, afraid she was about to fall over again.

'What's wrong?' He moved quickly, wrapping his arm around her waist to support her.

'I must have twisted my ankle. I can't put any weight on it.' She tried to take a step forward, which resulted in a sharp pain shooting up her leg. The adrenaline rush Seth had caused with his mouth-to-mouth technique must have temporarily blocked out the pain. She would've asked for a repeat prescription if she'd thought he'd oblige.

'You can't hobble around on that all day. We probably need to get it strapped up. Maybe we should head back?'

As well as wanting to spend more time with Seth, Kaja wasn't in a hurry to go back with her tail between her legs, or, in this case, her ankle in a plaster cast.

'We're closer to the site now than the hospital. I'll be fine.' She brushed off his concern and tried to walk on, grimacing through the pain but not yet ready to let go of her human crutch.

Seth huffed out a sigh. 'Sit down.'

He manoeuvred her over to an upturned tree trunk and made her sit while he wandered off. After a few minutes of sitting there on her own Kaja began to panic that he might have gone to get help. Visions of search teams swarming the woods looking for her made her regret this outing even if she had finally been able to kiss Seth again. She could only hope he wouldn't find himself in trouble when he reported back.

The sound she expected to hear next was helicopters or blaring sirens, not the rustle of leaves as Seth trudged back towards her swinging her heels in one hand.

'I'm not sure they'd suit you,' she said, trying to hide how inexplicably teary she was to see him, grateful he was going to help her find a way out of this mess she'd got herself into. He could easily have handed over responsibility to any one of the entourage paid to look after her.

'I'm not sure they go with a twisted ankle either but I brought them back for you.' He whacked them against the edge of the tree until the heels came off, making them into a pair of flats and leaving her wincing at the sacrifice.

It took everything she had not to squirm when he knelt down to take her foot in his hand. She was ticklish at the best of times but Seth touching her bare foot was too much to take. How often had he taken advantage of that weakness until she was screaming with laughter and they'd fallen into bed in a tangle of limbs? Except this time he was deadly serious as he examined her, showing no memory of those fun times that had always led to something more passionate.

'Can you move it? Good. It's a bit red but not too swollen. You probably need to rest it.'

'How am I going to do that? Hover?' Okay, her ego was as bruised as her ankle if he'd forgotten her little quirk so readily.

He turned around and crouched down. While he was giving her a good look at his tight backside, she wasn't sure what he was expecting her to do.

'Right, jump on.'

'Excuse me?' It was true she wanted to climb him like a tree but he'd made it abundantly clear that wasn't an option.

'You can't walk and taxis are scarce out here. Think of me as your trusty steed.' He whinnied and pawed the ground with his foot. Boy, she missed his silly sense of humour. It hadn't died after all. He must have buried it along with his feelings for her but the more time they spent together, the more she got to see flashes of the old Seth.

'You're kidding, right?' He couldn't possibly expect her to climb on his back and let him carry her not inconsiderable weight to their destination.

'Not at all.' He slapped his backside and crouched down a little more until his trousers were stretched tight around his peachy behind. 'Now climb on before I can't get up again.'

'Only if you're sure. I don't want us both lying crocked out here waiting for a rescue team to come and find us. Think of the scandal!' She shook her head, wondering how she'd found herself in such a ludicrous position. Kaja climbing onto the back of her father's transplant surgeon, barefoot and covered in grass stains, was a million-dollar photo op. Seth Davenport was making her reckless and she'd be lying if she said that wasn't the biggest thrill she'd had in years.

CHAPTER EIGHT

SETH'S PLAN TO break out of Kaja's claustrophobic existence with her in the hope it would provide some space had backfired spectacularly now she was clinging onto his back like a baby monkey.

'Are you comfy back there?'

'I wouldn't say "comfy", exactly, but you're saving my ankle. I'm not so sure about your back though.' She shifted her position to sit higher and strengthened her hold around him.

With the soft mounds of her breasts rubbing against him, legs wrapped territorially around his waist and cheek brushing against his, his back wasn't the part of his body he was worried about.

'Don't you worry about me. You're light as a feather.'

'Liar!' She slapped him playfully on the shoulder but made no attempt to disengage herself. Seth was simply glad he could do something to help. This whole sorry debacle had been his idea and now, not only were they probably causing mass panic back at the hospital, but she was hurt. Something he'd never seen coming. Along with that kiss.

He didn't know where he'd found the strength to end it but it had saved them both from making any further mistakes. Getting together again could only end in a mess and more heartache when he inevitably returned home to England. Perhaps that was part of the reason he'd agreed to come to her country when he knew he'd be the one leaving this time. Ensuring his departure meant there was no way she could hurt him. He hadn't counted on causing his own self-destruction by kissing her.

Now they'd crossed that boundary and let passion take over it was going to be difficult not to let it happen again.

The pilgrimage to her childhood hangout wasn't an easy one without a well-worn path to follow. There were dips and hills, rocky outcrops and streams to navigate along the way. As a reasonably fit adult man he would've struggled even without his Kaja backpack. It would've been even more of a trek for two young kids from the palace. He could only imagine the pressure of their heritage, which had driven them all the way out here on their own. It showed the strain she was currently under when this was the first place she thought of to escape to for a while.

'Oh, no. It looks like we're not the only ones visiting today.' Kaja pointed up ahead. Right beside the site of the crumbling grey ruins of a once bustling village was the juxtaposition of a bright red, super modern hatchback.

'Best case—they don't know who you are and we can hitch a lift back with them. Worst case—you let them take a few selfies and they give us a lift.' They'd had their adventure en route, rolling around in the grass together.

'I suppose so… In that case I should probably walk the rest of the way. We wouldn't want to draw any more attention than necessary.'

She had a point. Regardless if these other visitors knew they were in the presence of royalty or not, the sight of two people in medical attire piggybacking in from the woods was going to seem a little strange.

He crouched down to allow her to step away.

'Do I have to book a time slot for the tour or

can we do it now?' As keen as he was to get Kaja back for medical attention and prevent any further concern as to her whereabouts, he was curious about the place. From the day she'd left him it had struck him that he'd never known her at all. He'd learned something of her background having lived it himself these past few days, but hearing more about her childhood might provide him with better insight into what had made her who she was today.

'There's not much call for my services. I can't tell you a lot about the history of Tobel. I'm sorry to say that wasn't important to an impetuous nine-year-old. However, if you'd like to see the very spot where I first beat my big brother in an obstacle race, or hear about the time I befriended a stray dog and kept him as my secret pet, then I'm your girl.' She limped ahead of him, apparently eager to revisit this place that held such treasured memories for her.

'Sounds perfect.' This was what he'd wanted for her all along. A chance to forget everything going on at the hospital and simply enjoy herself.

Thankfully the occupants of the car were more interested in the picnic they'd spread out on the outer wall of the old village and didn't see them approach. Seth made a note to do the same with Amy when he got the chance. Perhaps not here, but he was sure she'd love a picnic out in the countryside.

Seth's stomach growled with hunger as they made their way along the cobbled street towards the tumbledown houses of yesteryear. He could see Kaja's foot already beginning to swell. Stumbling over this uneven ground with her foot wedged into broken shoes wasn't going to help. She'd be lucky if she could walk on it at all by the end of the day. Although, as she hovered in the doorway of one higgledy-piggledy building it was obvious she wanted to do some exploring before they thought about making their way home again.

'Is it the same as you remember?' There was a certain kind of beauty about a place where wild flowers were springing out of the glassless windows, the pale lemon and blues providing some colour against the grey stone. Nature had taken over from the last inhabitants and decorated accordingly. Even the weeds and moss that had set up home in every crack and groove of the crumbling structure had a certain aesthetic charm.

'A little more overgrown perhaps, but basically the same.' She ducked her head under the arched doorway and ventured inside with Seth following close behind.

'Smaller than I remember.' They walked through the remains of someone's house with only partial walls separating each of the rooms. 'I think the elements have taken their toll too.'

Seth could hear the tinge of sadness in her voice as she traced her hand over the faded mural barely there on what remained of the plaster. There were some flourishes and cornices left from what must have been a decorative abode at one time. Definitely a place where one could let their imagination run wild.

'Sometimes we look back on things with rose-tinted glasses. Reality doesn't always match up with the memories we might have embellished over the years.' Though, if this had been abandoned centuries ago he couldn't see it was in much better condition when Kaja and Bruno were here as children.

The look she gave him made him feel as

though he'd taken her favourite childhood toy and set fire to it.

'I'm sorry if meeting me again has been such a disappointment to you, Seth. Speaking for myself, I have no regrets about anything we've done. You met all the expectations I had based on my memories.' With that, she flounced out, leaving Seth scratching his head about what had caused the outburst. It took a minute too long for him to realise the misunderstanding.

'Wait… Kaja… I wasn't talking about us. I don't regret what happened between us back there either. If anything, being with you, kissing you, is even better than I remember.' He followed her into the next almost-room, her upset at believing he was unaffected by their tryst totally understandable.

She had her back to him, arms wrapped around her waist in a gesture of self-comfort that caused him physical pain on her behalf. He placed his hand on her elbow and gently turned her to face him.

'Hey, I was talking about the village, not us.' He gave her a soft smile, trying to coax one back in response. 'I didn't want to stop kissing you. That was the problem.'

Her mouth formed a perfect 'O'. 'Honestly?'

'Honestly.' He knew he shouldn't do it, yet Seth couldn't seem to stop himself from reaching out and tipping her chin up to make her look at him. The beautiful sad eyes and the pouting pink lips were too much for him to ignore.

He rested his lips on hers. Only for a second. Enough to comfort her and satisfy his need to feel her mouth against his one more time. He closed his eyes and blocked out the forsaken terrain around them, the soft touch of Kaja's lips transporting him to paradise instead.

It wasn't supposed to be a replay of their time on the forest floor, yet when Kaja sighed and let her arms fall away from their defensive position he wanted her closer. He pulled her body flush with his and that comforting kiss developed into a passionate display of his feelings for her. It was pointless denying it any more when he'd known from the second he'd set eyes on Kaja again he'd never stopped loving her. With Amy to take care of he'd been able to deny that fact and convince himself his heart only had room for his daughter. Now he was confronted with the person he'd so desperately wanted to share his life with and slowly rediscovering the woman he loved, those feelings refused to remain hidden.

They might not have a future together but he was willing to fully embrace the present.

Kaja was a fool. Why did she ever think she could live without this man and how had she managed it until now? It was only having him here in her world she understood what she was missing when his kisses were giving her life. She didn't care how stupid she'd been mistaking his comments about the ruins as a narrative on their relationship when it had prompted him into confessing his feelings for her. At least he still had some even if they weren't as strong as before. With her hands she reacquainted herself with the contours of his body while reuniting her tongue, her lips and her heart with his.

Seth held her, warming her back yet still managing to make her shiver. He was here, he was real, and, for now, all that mattered. When he slid a hand up inside her scrubs she held her breath, his palm grazing her ribs and reaching further to cup her breast. She let out a shaky breath as he brushed his thumb lightly across the silky material of her bra, bringing the sensitive peak of flesh to attention.

She wanted his touch, to feel skin on skin so badly she was practically begging him with her body. Grinding against him, she could feel his arousal standing proud and ready through the thin layer of clothing between them.

Seth groaned and in one swift move lifted her off her feet, hitched her legs up around his waist and carried her over to the recess at the window.

'Seth...we can't do this here.' Somewhere at the back of her mind beyond the rushing blood and carnal thoughts she remembered they had company outside.

'I know,' he said before claiming her again in another frantic coupling of mouths and tongues. Confirming he knew they couldn't get carried away any further than they already had but was as powerless as Kaja was in fighting this tidal wave of desire. Now it had broken free she didn't know how they were going to stem it again.

A loud rumble reverberated through the room, so strong it seemed to shake the very ground beneath them.

'I didn't know trains ran this far out.' Seth broke off the kiss, apparently as startled as she was by the loud sound suddenly approaching.

'They don't. There aren't any tracks out this way.' Come to think of it, the dirt roads out here wouldn't usually be travelled by any vehicles larger than the car parked outside.

It was only when the very walls of the building seemed to move with them that it dawned on her what could be causing the noise.

'Earthquake,' she shouted over the grinding noise coming from the earth below.

The warning came too late to get out of the seriously precarious structure as the underground monster roared its arrival. The ground undulated and warped as though they were on a roller-coaster ride they couldn't get off. Where once Kaja and Seth had been in the midst of a passionate embrace, now they were clinging to one another in an attempt to stay upright.

'Aren't we supposed to go and stand in the doorway?' he shouted, trying to pull her in that direction.

She resisted, shaking her head. 'It's not stable enough.'

With that, the world seemed to cave in around

them. Walls were collapsing, including the arched doorway, their only means of escape. Plaster began to fall in chunks around them. Seth covered her head with his hands and pulled her down onto the ground with him, using his body as a shield to protect her from the falling debris.

Kaja had never been in an actual earthquake as there hadn't been one here in living history but she had a vague recollection of what to do should one ever occur. She thanked the heavens she had Seth with her providing comfort in a terrifying situation. He was the only stable thing she had to hold onto at a time when she couldn't even rely on the *terra*-not-so-*firma*.

She scrunched her eyes shut, her head against Seth's chest. Unfortunately, she couldn't turn off the sound, every dull crack and thud as debris rained down reminding her how very small and fragile they were. There was every chance that neither of them would come out of this when there seemed no end in sight to the destruction happening right on top of them.

'We are going to get out of this, Kaja.' He kissed her forehead, providing a moment of calm tenderness in the midst of such overwhelming chaos. Then he added, 'We have to,' with such a determined look on his face she believed him.

Amy. He was thinking about his daughter, of course he was. With that came the horror of what was happening to all of their loved ones: her father, Bruno, Fatima. There was no time to descend into hysterics and what ifs as another crash of rubble sounded. Along with a sharp curse from Seth.

'Are you all right?' She'd felt him tense at the same time as the new fall of debris and poked her head out of her Seth cocoon to make sure he was all right when he was bearing the brunt of the blows to save her.

'I'm fine.' He was much too abrupt to convince her.

Sure enough as she reached up to brush the dusty swoop of hair from his face, her fingers encountered a sticky patch of blood at his temple.

'You're bleeding.'

'I'll live.' He kept turning his head and trying to put her off but she could see the cut and wasn't going to rest until she examined it. A head injury wasn't something to simply brush off. Thankfully there was only a trickle of blood so it likely didn't need stitches.

'You'd better.'

As quickly as the world seemed to erupt around them, the upheaval subsided again, the roar fading along with that sensation of being at sea. It couldn't have lasted for any more than a minute but it had been an eternity waiting to find out if they'd live through it all.

'Quick, let's get out of here in case there are any aftershocks.' Paying no heed to his injury Seth grabbed her hands and pulled her to her feet.

Her legs wobbled as though she'd spent months on the ocean and had just set foot on land again. It was difficult to see, darkness having descended along with a curtain of dust, but when it cleared the state of the devastation was obvious.

'The door's gone.' The archway, along with most of the walls that had been holding up what was left of the building, were a mound of slate and brick. Looking around, she could see how lucky they'd been in the grand scheme of things.

They could have been buried alive. She shuddered when she recalled how Seth had cradled her with his body. She would never have forgiven herself if he'd died sacrificing himself to save her.

Unfortunately, they discovered none of the original exits had survived. They'd literally been entombed in her favourite childhood playground. The angle one of the beams had fallen and thankfully created a pocket of air around them so they had space to move.

Seth began shifting the biggest obstacles, kicking and pushing until there was a large enough gap for them to break out of their stone igloo.

'C'mon!' There was an understandable urgency in him as he reached back for her. They had to get out into an open space before any further ructions erased any chance of them escaping.

Kaja followed through the tunnel he was burrowing through the rubble, incapable of speech until they saw daylight and Seth pulled her through to safety. They collapsed in a heap on the grass outside, breathing heavily from a combination of physical exertion and fear.

'I don't even know where we are.' It was

disorienting when nothing looked the same as when they'd first arrived. Most of the old buildings were now reduced to little more than a pile of rubble amidst a cloud of dirt and debris. She didn't know why she wasn't a hysterical mess screaming and crying after the trauma of what they'd been through. What they might still go through. She was clearly in some sort of shock, trying to process what had just happened.

Seth stood up and paced around. Even he didn't look quite as steady on his feet as usual. Kaja wasn't sure she could even stand again.

'Come over here and let me look at that head injury.'

'It's nothing.'

'Let me be the judge of that,' she insisted, unwilling to take any chances in the circumstances.

He reluctantly came back to her, not wanting a fuss but bending down so she could make a closer inspection of the wound. Using the hem of her top, she gently dabbed at the blood, cleaning the site enough so she could see the extent of the cut. 'It's not too deep. I think it'll heal itself. No need for improvised stitching.'

'Good. Can we focus on something more important now?'

'There's no need to be tetchy. I just want to make sure you're safe.'

'I know. Sorry. I think we came out the back of the house. We should be safe out here away from any more falling wreckage.'

Kaja glanced back at the way they'd come. From this vantage point on the hill she could see plumes of smoke in the city and now the thundering sound had stopped she could hear sirens going off everywhere. They were isolated with no idea what had gone on in the rest of the country or who was hurt. It was part luck, part Seth that had saved them, but there was no way of knowing what was happening elsewhere to everyone else or how bad the devastation.

Seth had the same thought as he pulled his phone from his pocket. They both waited as the call rang out until they eventually heard Fatima's voice.

'Are you and Amy okay?'

'Yes, Mr Davenport. We hid under the dining table. No one got hurt. How are you and Miss Kaja?'

The line went dead and Seth tried again and again to reconnect without success. 'I don't have any signal. At a guess I'd say all lines are down and the power's probably out.'

'At least we know they're all right. Fatima will keep Amy safe. What about Papa and Bruno…? Seth, what'll happen to them?' Her heart was in an ever-tightening vice as she thought back to all the machinery monitoring them. Her father especially, who was so vulnerable after the transplant.

Seth walked back to her and took a seat on the grass again. 'Hey, they'll be fine. Surely the hospital will have emergency power for a situation like this?'

She knew they would, yet it wasn't any consolation. Logic wasn't getting a look-in when emotions and her imagination were running wild. 'We have to get back.'

'Don't you think I know that?' he snapped. 'My daughter is miles away, frightened, without her daddy but we can't go anywhere. We'd be taking a risk going back through the trees if there are further aftershocks. The same if we take the road. We could get hit by all sorts of debris and there's always a chance the roads themselves could open up. That's if you hadn't hurt your ankle and were capable of walking back. We're going to have to wait this out. No matter how hard it is not knowing what's happening to our loved ones.'

He was trying so hard to be strong for her but Kaja could hear how choked up he was about Amy. The way he'd protected her and dug them out of that house with his bare hands…she knew he'd have done the same for his daughter. This separation had to be so much worse for him.

She reached across and squeezed his hand. 'Fatima will take care of her and the palace is one of the safest places to be. When it was remodelled for our family it was extensively renovated to withstand any eventuality.'

'It's just…there's so much in that house which could fall on her. The heavy furniture, the chandeliers…she's only a little thing.' The catch in his voice threatened to undo them both. Kaja needed him to stay strong or she'd lose it altogether too.

'Fatima knew to take cover as soon as the earthquake hit and they're fine. I'm sure the rest of the staff will be taking care of them too.'

'You're right. If we start thinking the worst we'll go around the bend. We need to focus on us for now. Until we can get back and do something to help.'

Good. Seth was taking back control. That made it easier for her to hold it together too.

'That siren sounds awfully close.' She couldn't help but hope someone knew where they were and had sent the emergency services to their rescue.

Seth scrambled to his feet. 'It's a car alarm.'

'The tourists. Maybe we can get a ride back with them.' The notion that they had a solution right here galvanised her back into action too. She tried not to think about the pain in her ankle returning now that the adrenaline had worn off. With any luck she wouldn't have to walk much further.

They followed the blaring noise and the flashing lights back to where the car was parked. The windows were smashed, glass everywhere, but it was still standing.

'Where did they go?' She looked around but there was no sign of the family who'd been sitting nearby. It felt as though the roller coaster went into free fall again, leaving her stomach somewhere on the ground.

'What if they're in there?' Seth voiced her fear as he looked back towards the empty skyline where the village had once stood.

Neither of them wanted to venture back there for their own sake but they were both medics and knew it had to be done.

CHAPTER NINE

'YOU STAY HERE. I'll go and look for them.'

'Like hell. I'm coming with you.' There was no way she was going to let him go back in there alone. If the past few minutes had shown her anything it was that they needed each other to survive and she wasn't going to stand back and let him put himself in danger.

Seth opened his mouth to protest and she folded her arms across her chest and pursed her lips. He wisely closed his mouth again and headed back towards the devastated village they'd literally just crawled out from.

'Hello? Is there anybody here?' he called as they walked into the courtyard that had once been the centre of the village. Now it was simply the epicentre of the destruction.

Any bright colour nature had once displayed had been obliterated by layers of grey as far as the eye could see. Glancing at what little was left of the buildings, Kaja realised how incredibly lucky they'd been. The house they'd wandered into was unrecognisable as a structure at all, her beloved mural now nothing but a few painted bricks scattered here and there.

'Maybe they ran off when it started?' Optimistic, perhaps, but she really didn't want Seth putting himself in jeopardy again for anyone.

'They wouldn't have had time to get very far and there's no one to be seen for miles out here.' Undeterred by the resounding silence, he kept walking further into the danger zone.

Kaja took a deep breath, refusing to let him go it alone but not without some trepidation. The next time the earth shook they mightn't be so fortunate.

'Hello? Can anyone hear us?' He put his hands to his mouth to amplify his plea for signs of life. With the car alarm still blaring in the background it was difficult to hear anything else. The place had a distinct Pompeii vibe. How Kaja imagined it after everything had been wiped out by Vesuvius.

They climbed up what felt like two storeys of wreckage listening for anything to indicate there was someone here who needed their help.

Kaja thought she heard movement where the

row of houses opposite the one they'd been inside had once stood.

'Seth! Over here.' She moved closer to investigate and beckoned him over. They began excavating the site on their hands and knees, certain there was someone beneath the remains.

'We're going to get you out,' Kaja called out, trying to provide some reassurance to whoever was trapped.

They heard whimpering far below and Seth became a man possessed, tearing away boulders with his bare hands, sweat trickling down his face. Both of them were covered in dirt, skin and nails torn to shreds before they made any progress. The small gap they managed to open up provided a peephole where Kaja could see the tear-streaked face of the little girl who'd been picnicking with her family staring back at her.

She sat back on her heels, stunned at the sight of the frightened child buried alive. It took Seth a heartbeat too before he resumed scrabbling at the rocks in desperation and she knew he was thinking this could easily have been his daughter.

'We'll get you out, honey. Is there anyone else

with you?' Kaja kept talking, getting the child to focus on her as the rocky world around her shifted once more.

The little girl nodded her head. Not a good sign. There had been a family, parents and a child enjoying the afternoon sunshine, and now only silence.

Kaja had to look away so the little girl wouldn't see her welling up. She was bound to be terrified enough without having an adult making things worse.

All of a sudden Seth stopped digging and sat up.

'What is it? What's wrong?'

'Shh! I thought I heard something over there.' He pointed to a spot close to him and they took a breather, listening until they heard a faint cry for help.

Seth glanced at the place where the little girl was waiting to be rescued, then back to where they'd located a new survivor.

'Go. I'll get her.' He'd already done most of the heavy lifting and the little girl was okay as far as they could tell. If there was someone else buried here Seth could rescue her and Kaja would concentrate on the child.

He didn't waste any time debating the subject, having the same confidence in her capabilities as she had in his.

Kaja cleared the obstacles as quickly and as deftly as she could. Hearing Seth murmur to the woman who was stuck down there was comforting and she believed every word he said about getting everyone out safely.

She was lying across the rubble now, stones and bricks jabbing into her ribs and every other part of her body in contact with the jagged floor beneath her.

'Here's my hand, honey. Can you grab it? Good girl.' Her cheek was practically embedded with part of the village landscape as she reached down through the gap. Even if she couldn't get the girl out right away she could assure her she wouldn't let go of her until someone did.

'Okay, sweetie, hold on with both hands and I'll pull you out of there.'

Although she was only a little thing, Kaja was sure she was going to dislocate both shoulders with the strain of wrenching her up through the hole alone.

'If you could put your foot on that rock…

good girl.' With one last heave she pulled the child free and collapsed on the uneven ground, panting for breath.

Once she managed to control her breathing Kaja turned to check on the little girl. 'Are you hurt anywhere?'

She shook her head. Eyes wide with fear, face stained with dirt and clothes torn, she resembled a Victorian street urchin. Not someone who only a short time ago had been having the time of her life with her family. Kaja's heart went out to her, hoping she'd be reunited with them soon.

She remembered the child had indicated someone else was down there with her but Kaja hadn't seen or heard anything other than the debris continuing to fall.

'Is there someone else down there?'

She nodded.

'Are they awake?'

She shook her head. Kaja understood she was in shock but she could really use some help to establish who was down there and in what condition. With Seth still bulldozing his way through the adjacent site it was down to her to locate any further survivors and get to them as soon as possible.

If there was someone else stuck down there she wasn't going to be able to get them out herself. Then again, she couldn't call Seth away from his task until she knew what they were up against.

'I'm going to go down and see if I can help. I need you to run over to that man there and he'll keep you safe until I come back up. Okay?'

Another nod. If anything happened while she was down there she knew Seth would get this little one to safety. There was a slight hesitation but Kaja assured her she'd join her soon. She took a deep breath to steel herself before she climbed into the gap they'd made in the rubble. It was a tight squeeze but the discomfort as she shimmied down was bearable. Whoever was down here had surely endured worse.

She dropped onto the ledge accessible through the new skylight they'd installed. From there she had to pick her way carefully down the loose stones and step down onto the ground. 'Hello? Is there someone down here? I got your daughter out. She's safe. Can you make a noise so I can find you?' The only sound she could hear was Seth's nearby excavation work.

It was dark and ominous in the depths of the devastated building. There was every chance the whole lot could come down on her at any time as she moved from room to room, climbing over mounds of rock. Her ankle screamed every time she jarred it on an uneven surface but she persevered.

When she came to the area of the building that seemed to have suffered the brunt of the damage, making it largely inaccessible, she was ready to give up the quest. Except as Kaja went to leave she spotted a flash of colour breaking through the grey. She bent down to take a closer look and there, buried in the landslide, was the very definite shape of an adult male whose bright Hawaiian shirt might have just saved his life.

'Can you hear me?' Kaja began to move the rocks around the rest of his body, careful not to knock anything more on top of him. His face was turned away from her but when she checked his wrist she could feel a rapid pulse beating against her fingers. It was a relief to know he was still alive but a fast heartbeat could also be an indication of serious injury. She needed a better look but he was unconscious and there was no way she could move him on her own when he was pinned under several large boulders.

'What the hell do you think you're doing coming down here on your own and scaring me half to death?' Seth's disapproval boomed around the enclosed space and gave Kaja such a fright her heart nearly popped out of her chest. Any more surprises today and she'd find herself in a hospital bed along with the rest of her family.

'There's a man trapped under the rocks.' She ignored his irritation at her to concentrate on the important matter at hand.

He came over to help but not without muttering about how stupid she was for putting herself in danger. As though he wouldn't have done exactly the same thing.

'He hasn't gained consciousness since I found him and his pulse is too fast for my liking.'

'We're going to have to get him out of here.'

'What about the woman you were helping?' She was almost afraid to ask in case the latest rescue attempt hadn't been successful.

'She's fine. A few cuts and bruises but she's with her daughter now. It was her who directed me over here. When I couldn't find you…' His face was dark. He was angry with her and it was only now she could see what it would've looked like when she disappeared. The last time he'd seen her she'd been digging in the rubble. A few minutes later she'd vanished, with only a hole remaining where she'd once stood.

'Sorry. I wasn't thinking about anything other than helping.'

'Right, well, no more disappearing acts. I don't think my heart can take it.'

It was a throwaway comment but the sentiment behind it meant the world. He was worried about her. As he'd so gallantly displayed during the earthquake, he cared. She wasn't going to let that slip through her hands again but they could talk about that when this crisis was over.

'First things first, we need to move him.' This guy was twice her size and she had been foolish to think she could do that on her own. It remained to be seen if they could do it now.

It would've been preferable for them to stabilise him with a neck brace and a back board until he had his injuries assessed properly in hospital. There was a danger of paralysis but life came before injury and getting him out of here was crucial to his survival. They couldn't risk another rock slide in here in case it injured him further. Crush injuries could prove lethal unless promptly treated.

Kaja pulled her ponytail loose and used the hair tie to apply a tourniquet above the injury site prior to moving the rock. 'Hopefully that will prevent the release of toxins into his bloodstream.'

Once she had limited the blood flow to the injured leg, Seth jumped over to try and shift the weight hampering their progress. Working together like this was reminiscent of those busy nights in A & E when their paths had occasionally crossed during an emergency. It was the same rush of adrenaline and understanding of each other's roles that made them such a good team. That didn't always happen with fellow surgeons and was probably more to do with their genuine affection and respect for one another.

'I'm…not…sure… I…can…lift…it.' Regardless that Seth was bound to be exhausted she could hear the effort he was putting in attempting to dislodge the obstacle.

'If you can shift it a fraction, maybe I could drag him out from under it.' Kaja grabbed the shoulders of the gawdy shirt and got ready to pull him free.

Seth manoeuvred himself between the man and the boulder and with a huff of breath braced his back against the rock to lever it off. His legs were shaking and his face was a violent shade of red with the strain he was putting on his body.

'I've got him.' Kaja hauled him out while Seth took the weight of the rock. Once he was free Seth let out a grunt and dropped the boulder as gently as he could without dislodging any more stones.

'His pallor is a little blue. A direct trauma to his chest during the rock fall could have fractured his ribs and punctured his lung.' Kaja had done her best not to jolt the man too much as she'd wiggled him free but there was no way of telling how much internal damage might have been caused during his ordeal. If air had collected in the space between the layers of tissue lining his lungs it would prevent them from expanding properly.

She put her ear down to the man's chest to listen to his breathing and the short, gurgling breaths did nothing to relieve her anxiety. 'We could be dealing with a traumatic pneumothorax. If we don't release that pressure he could suffocate.'

'We don't have the luxury of medical facilities to help him or even access to a chest tube to help drain the air.'

'We'll have to improvise. I don't suppose you've got a pen on you?' She was only half joking, having seen this scene dramatised in a number of TV programmes. In real life it was a risky move with too much room for error. However, in these circumstances they were out of options.

Seth emptied the contents of his trouser pockets into his hands. While there wasn't a pen, he did have a mini pocket knife. Literally, a lifesaver.

'What's in this?' Kaja pointed to a small metal tin he held.

'It's a reusable metal straw. Amy's very insistent on using it instead of the plastic ones, which could find their way into the ocean and choke a turtle or something.'

'Good girl. That has to be an improvement on an empty pen barrel. Although, I think you might have to buy a new one after this.'

'No worries. I keep it scrupulously clean so it should be sterile enough to use.' The tin contained the tiniest brushes Kaja had ever seen so she didn't doubt him.

'Okay. I'm going to make a small incision with the knife for access and insert the straw to let the air out. That should let the lungs expand again and help him breathe.' These weren't the ideal conditions to work in with so much dust and dirt but they were far from help and if they did nothing, this man wouldn't make it. Neither she nor Seth would stand and watch him die without trying their best to save him.

Seth opened up the man's shirt, exposing the torso so Kaja could work. 'You can do this.' Seth urged her on as the butterflies in her stomach threatened to fight their way up and out.

In England she'd thrived with every emergency that came through the hospital doors. Although she did her best to keep her hand in at the hospital here, this felt as though it was the first time she'd really been tested on her home turf.

She could do this, she knew that deep down, but she was thankful for his encouragement. Any other capable surgeon might have tried to muscle their way in and take over. It was reassuring that he believed in her as much as he always had where her job was concerned. They worked as easily together as ever, happy to let the other take the lead when necessary. Much like their relationship. Seth had never put any pressure on her to do anything, letting her do everything at her own pace so she was comfortable. Including moving in with him, which had taken her some time to agree to as it had seemed such a huge step at the time. Seth had always believed in her and, despite everything since, that had never changed.

Kaja felt her way along the patient's torso until she was sure she'd located a gap between the lower ribs. A deep breath to steady herself and she plunged the tip of the small knife in, allowing the trapped air to escape. Seth passed her the metal straw to insert in order to keep the airway open.

'Ideally, we'd have some surgical tape to keep that in place.'

'Sorry. I don't keep that on me but it's a fold-away straw. Perhaps if you retract it as much as possible there's less chance of it falling out.' He held the base of the straw steady in the site, letting her push it down as far as it would go.

Kaja tried to be as gentle as possible when there was no pain relief available but their patient remained unconscious throughout.

It was vital they got him to hospital as soon as possible so surgeons could use the appropriate equipment to repair the injuries but how? They were both running on empty, he was a big guy and there was no way they could carry him back up the way they'd come in.

'We need to find a way to keep him lying flat and stretcher him out.'

'Easier said than done, Seth.' If they'd had access to the emergency services that wouldn't have been too much of a problem. However, this emergency rescue rested solely on their shoulders.

'We should be able to tunnel our way back out to the main courtyard.

Kaja didn't know if he was trying to convince

her or himself. Even if they managed to get him out there were still risks of him suffering from infection, inflammation or fluid developing in the lung. At worst, cardiac arrest. For everyone's safety they needed to get out of here before they were hit by any further complications.

'Should we enlist some extra help from outside?' The only other available pairs of hands belonged to the two they'd just dug out but they had run out of options.

'Good idea. I'll go back out, try and pinpoint where we need to go and get his family to start working from the other side. At least that way we might cut down on the time.' Along with the effort required.

She waited for Seth to climb back out of the hole above and listened for him on the other side. Eventually, she heard him shouting. 'Kaja, let me know when we're close.'

'Kaja?' Seth shouted again, closer this time.

She moved as close to the outer wall as she could. 'I'm here, Seth.'

That all too familiar sound of scraping and tumbling rocks began again and she waited for those on the outside to clear a path to them. It was hard manual labour in the heat as well as stressful. She was beginning to wonder if the nightmare would ever end. It seemed as though they'd been living on the edge of hell for hours now when in reality it was probably only a matter of minutes.

After a while she could see a chink of light through the gap made in the outer wall. It grew steadily bigger until Seth was visible on the other side working alongside the woman he'd rescued from nearby. Even the little girl was helping to move the rocks aside.

Once there was enough room for Seth to pass through he joined her inside and between them they lifted the incapacitated man. Seth grabbed him under the armpits and Kaja grabbed his legs. He was heavy but they were careful not to knock out the straw chest tube, carrying their patient until he was free from the danger of being hit by any more falling debris.

'Do you have the keys to the car?' Seth asked the woman crying over her husband's battered body, stroking his face and begging him to wake up.

'My husband had them.' She sniffed and searched his pockets. There was a collective sigh of relief when she produced them. They would never have found them if they'd fallen out along the way.

'We need to get him to the hospital for X-rays. He might have a punctured lung so we've put this tube in to help him breathe better. Can you drive?' Kaja asked the woman, aware that this car was the only available means to get back and they didn't even know if it was drivable.

She nodded, pulling her little girl close.

'Go and get the car and bring it back here. We're going to have to put the back seat down and lay him flat in the back to prevent as much movement as we can. You'll have to keep an eye on that straw to make sure it's not dislodged on the journey.' Seth issued the orders with so much authority no one questioned him.

It was a blessed relief when the car alarm was turned off. Once the car was reversed in as close as they could get it, Seth cleared the glass from the interior.

They lifted their patient again, Seth backing up inside the car so they could fit him comfortably on the passenger side lengthways.

Kaja gave the terrified wife directions to the hospital as she clutched the steering wheel.

'Try to avoid driving close to any trees or any other large structures in case there are any aftershocks.'

'I think you should squeeze in there too, Kaja.' Seth's last-minute suggestion threw her so much she nearly lost her professional composure.

'No!'

'You're hurt. It makes sense for one of us to try and get help. I'll be fine here. There's nothing to stop me walking back along the road.' He was being sincere but that only strengthened her resolve to stay with him.

'There's no way I'm leaving you behind.' She'd done that once too often.

'Kaja—'

She ignored his plea and put her own to the woman in the car. 'If you could let someone know we're out here and need transport back, we'd be very grateful.'

'I'll do my best. Thank you so much for everything.'

They said their goodbyes and wished each other luck before Kaja and Seth waved the family off.

'You didn't have to stay with me.'

'Yes, I did.'

He sighed, apparently getting the message she wasn't going to back down over that. She was done being selfish.

'You were amazing back there,' he told her, downplaying the lives he'd rescued too.

'All part of the day job. It felt good to be back in the thick of things. Although, I'd have preferred to have been working in a more traditional setting.'

'That makes two of us. Still, if we hadn't been here that family wouldn't have got out alive.'

The thought made her shiver but it also gave her a boost knowing she'd made a difference today. Her work as a surgeon was more important than anything she did in a royal capacity and infinitely more fulfilling. A matter she couldn't ignore now their close call with death was making her reassess the choices she'd made and the unhappy life she'd been living as a result.

CHAPTER TEN

'YOU KNOW, YOU could've increased our chances of getting rescued if you'd told her who you were,' Seth said with a bemused grin.

Kaja wrinkled her nose at the suggestion. 'I wouldn't do that. In this situation we're all in the same boat. It wouldn't be fair to divert emergency services when they're needed much more elsewhere. We're not hurt, we're safe. If she passes the message on someone will get to us eventually.'

She didn't count her ankle as a serious injury when it was neither life-threatening nor caused by the earthquake. Even if it was throbbing like hell.

'My Kaja. Always putting other people first.' Seth put an arm around her shoulders and kissed her forehead.

She wanted to fall into his arms and pick up where they'd left off before nature had roared its disapproval but so much had happened since then. Seth's worry for his daughter, for all those caught in the quake, had overridden any discussion about their relationship. Even if there was some way of sustaining a long-distance romance the issue over her divided loyalties remained. They were both going to have to make big life changes to make it work. In her case there was one huge problem that couldn't be overcome with desire alone.

He led her outside the perimeter of the village back onto safer ground out in the open.

Kaja spotted some objects lying in the field behind the ruins of the wall where the family had been having their lunch earlier. They walked over to find a rolled-up blanket and the remains of their picnic in a cooler box.

'Okay, we've got a bottle of water, an orange and some breadsticks.' Seth discarded the half-eaten sandwich and the dubious-looking yoghurt back in the cooler. Hopefully they'd get picked up before they had to resort to eating any of that.

He spread the tartan rug out on the grass for them to sit on. The light was beginning to fade as the evening drew in but thankfully it was still warm. If help didn't arrive soon there was every chance they'd be spending the night under the stars.

'Do we need to ration the food or can we feast?' Kaja teased as she held up the meagre provisions they'd scavenged.

'I'm willing to take the chance we're going to get rescued before we resort to divvying out crumbs. We haven't eaten since breakfast and I think we deserve a little treat. Now, would madam prefer an orange segment or the bread course first?'

'Mmm, I think I'd like to start with some orange, thank you.'

It was ridiculous sitting out here in the aftermath of an earthquake joking and pretending that things were all right but Seth wanted to make Kaja laugh rather than have her dwell on things beyond their control.

He didn't want to think about what could have happened to her back there either, when he'd come close to losing her. For ever this time. Her stubborn refusal to go with the others and stay with him had been touching. If she'd been more concerned with her own welfare she would've gone to the hospital. It proved, along with their earlier kisses, that he was more to her than a house guest or simply here for her father's benefit. He didn't know what that meant for them but, for now, he was happy they were together.

He peeled the orange for her, the sweet, refreshing scent of citrus preferable to the earthiness and dust they'd been breathing in since the quake hit.

Kaja popped a piece in her mouth and closed her eyes. 'Mmm. That tastes so good.'

He had to agree. On a day like today one small piece of fruit had suddenly become the best thing he'd ever eaten.

'Could I also recommend our house water to accompany the dish?' He opened the bottled water and offered her the first sip.

Kaja waved the bottle under her nose, took a drink and swilled the water around her mouth before swallowing. They were being silly. A kind of hysterical reaction to the trauma they'd just been through. It didn't last and they fell silent as they devoured the rest of the orange. His body was becoming weary now and his muscles were aching after all the heavy lifting he'd been doing. He lay down on the blanket leaving Kaja sitting up, nursing what was left of the bottle of water.

Only moments after closing his eyes there was that ominous rumbling below the earth. He felt Kaja tense beside him, as the ground shook and forced them back onto that unwanted fair-ground ride. It was impossible to remain flat when every tremor was reverberating through his body. He sat up and hugged Kaja until the world stopped trembling. It was all he could do to protect her out here.

'I think that's it over for now.' It was little re-assurance to her, he was sure, as they could still hear the sound of loose rocks tumbling nearby and see the new fissures opening up in the road ahead. 'Hopefully the family got to the hospi-tal before the aftershock. Although I'm sure it won't be the last.'

Kaja was quiet. Too quiet. Then it seemed as though a mini earthquake of emotions began inside her. The shaking came first, her shoul-ders heaving beneath his arm, but it was the sobbing that took him most by surprise.

'Hey, we're gonna be okay. That one was quick.'

He cursed himself for being the voice of

doom predicting more nerve-shattering after-shocks even though it was the truth. Usually Kaja preferred that kind of straight talking but perhaps under the circumstances she was a bit more fragile. From now on he'd be careful not to upset her. Not when he'd been drawing from her strength to keep going throughout this ordeal.

She leaned back into his chest, content to let him hold her. A cry for help in itself for someone who'd single-handedly waded into a collapsed building to rescue a man twice her size. Kaja was a strong woman who didn't accept help easily, as he'd discovered in those early days of working together when he'd tried to get closer to her. It took her a long time to trust anyone but he'd been persistent, willing to put in the time getting to know her when he'd been so entranced by the newest medic on the block. There'd been something so endearingly naive about her beyond the efficient, focused surgeon. Of course, now he knew why she wasn't as worldly wise as some of her counterparts and the reasons she liked her privacy so much.

He let her cry it out until they were both soaked with her tears and she was ready to talk.

'It's just too much to take in. We could've been killed. We still could.' Her face crumpled again as she contemplated their fate.

Seth didn't want to upset her but neither would he lie to her. There was no way of knowing how this would end for anyone. It was probably the shock setting in that was making them both so emotional. Without the drama and distraction of saving others they had time to replay events and think about their loved ones. If he let himself go down that rabbit hole and start catastrophising what was going on with Amy back at the palace he'd be sobbing too.

'We're still here,' he reminded her. 'Mother Nature has tried twice to take us out and failed. Hopefully she'll take the hint and leave us alone for a bit, yeah?'

She managed a half-hearted smile. 'Thanks for today. I know this wasn't what you had in mind when you suggested an adventure but I'm glad I'm with you.'

'Me too.' He snuggled in closer to Kaja, nuzzling his nose into the curtain of her hair. In the short space of time since they'd got to know each other again she'd quickly become an important element of his life once more. As if those intervening years had never happened and their life together had carried on where it had left off. Easy to do out here where there were no reminders of how different her world was or the relationships they'd had after their separation.

He breathed her in, her hair smelling of dust and earth but also the sweet floral perfume that was unmistakably Kaja. If he closed his eyes he could almost believe they were back in their house in Cambridge.

She turned her head so he was almost nose to nose with her now. Eyes open, lips parted, their breath mingling as they mirrored each other. Seth didn't know who made the first move, they were so in tune with each other, gravitating towards that kiss they both knew was coming.

Here, now, she was all that mattered to him. She was everything reminding him he was still alive. He kissed her as though it might be for the last time. Hard and passionate enough that he forgot to breathe. They fell down onto the rug still wrapped up in one another, hands tugging at one another's clothes, impatience erasing all logical thought. Seth wanted Kaja as he'd never wanted any woman before. He needed that reaffirmation that she was back in his life, that she hadn't fallen out of love with him after all and that she wanted him too. She was telling him that with her words and every stroke of her tongue against his.

He slid her top over her head but his shirt buttons proved more time-consuming. After fumbling with the first two she gave a frustrated groan and yanked the shirt open. The night air cooled Seth's fevered skin but not for long when Kaja trailed first her fingers then her tongue down his chest and lower. Now his breaths were coming in excited pants as she snapped open the buttons on his fly and left him in no doubt what it was she was expecting from him. Seth flipped her over onto her back to slow things down. He hadn't been with anyone since Paula and he needed to regain some control over his body as well as savour every moment with Kaja while he could.

Not that she was doing anything to help that vow as she wriggled out of her scrub trousers so she was lying beneath him clad only in skimpy black silk lingerie.

'You're beautiful.' The sentiment slipped

from his lips. She didn't need the expensive clothes or the royal title to be anyone special when to him she was the most beautiful woman on the planet.

'And you're still dressed,' she purred as she grabbed him by the collar and pulled him back down into another brain-melting kiss. If this was all she wanted from him for now he wasn't going to turn her down. This memory would be a more pleasant one than the last night they'd spent together. Only this time he'd be the one leaving and hopefully on better terms.

This was madness. Kaja knew it yet she didn't want her sanity to return any time soon. She'd never felt more alive than she did right now getting naked with Seth in the open air. They had all the reasons in the world not to pursue a relationship further but none that could convince her that sleeping with him here and now was the wrong thing to do. They'd been through a lot together and in the scheme of things it seemed silly not to act on these feelings they had for one another. Life was too short to deny themselves some pleasure. She didn't want to wait any longer.

Seth was taking his sweet time kissing the skin along her neck and across her clavicle, until Kaja was aching with need. She undid her bra and tossed it aside, revelling in the hungry look he gave her as she exposed her breasts to his gaze. He cupped her soft mounds in the palms of his large hands, kneading and kissing the sensitive flesh until her nipples were throbbing in anticipation of his touch. When he pinched them between his fingers and thumbs she bucked off the ground, that painful ecstasy only furthering her desire. He flicked his tongue over the taut tips, teasing her, the glint in his eye promising her so much more. When he took her in his mouth and sucked, he delivered on that promise.

Arousal swept away the very last of her inhibitions and patience. She pushed down his briefs and pressed her body against his engorged erection. It was the final straw for Seth too. He let out a primal grunt, pulled the last of her underwear away and plunged inside her.

Kaja's gasp was one of surprise and satisfaction that she'd finally got what she wanted. They paused for a second, their bodies both adjusting as they joined together.

His eyes searching hers. 'Are you okay?'

'Uh-huh.' She nodded, though she doubted she'd ever be okay again after this. It was such a wanton display of need and raw passion she knew nothing or no one else could ever surpass it. He kissed her softly on the lips then began moving rhythmically inside her, reminding her how good they could be together. She rocked her hips against his, losing herself in that full feeling every time he rammed her to the hilt.

'I've missed you so much,' he whispered in her ear, sending tiny shivers of delight up the back of her neck both from what he was saying and doing to her.

She was incapable of talking right now. Even if she hadn't been in the throes of ecstasy the sincerity of his words would've rendered her speechless. He should hate her for the way she'd lied to him, the manner in which she'd left him, but most of all for denying them a future together. Hearing him say those words, knowing he would've forgiven her and taken her back, made those bad-decision years all the more painful. At least she had him in this moment and she intended to make the most of their time together.

Kaja clung to him, never wanting to let go as he took her higher and higher on that wave of pure bliss. Why had she ever given up on this? On them? Especially when...

Oh.

All regrets and tears, any thoughts at all, were now simply background noise as Seth set off a fireworks display inside her. Lights flashed behind her eyelids as a succession of delicious explosions detonated in her body, all triggered by what Seth was doing to her. Her orgasm was prolonged and repeated over and over again as he continued working his magic, not letting up on his now frantic pace until she was limp and sated beneath him. Totally exhausted and completely satisfied. Only then did he give into his own fierce need, his climax seeming as overwhelming as hers when he cried out into the night.

When she was able to see straight and breathe again—albeit hindered by the gorgeous hunk currently sprawled across her body—she fully appreciated the beauty of the moment. '*Belle Crepuscolo*—it means beautiful twilight.'

A dazed Seth looked down at her, his hair flopping over his face and his eyelids heavy with exhaustion. He kissed her again and though she knew she was getting carried away by the romance of the moment she couldn't help it.

'This is madness,' she reminded them both.

'What, sleeping with me?' He genuinely looked hurt but her comment had absolutely nothing to do with sex.

'Of course not. You know that was amazing.' Despite everything they'd just done she felt her skin flush at acknowledging the mere memory. She wrapped her arms around his neck, pressing her chest to his and nibbling his earlobe. 'I mean the fact we're lying naked in the middle of a field.'

But she didn't care. Being with Seth was her happy place.

'It's certainly a night to remember,' he said with a grin.

'I wish it could be like this all the time. Only without the whole earthquake and danger-to-life thing.'

'I know what you mean.' He lifted her hand to his mouth and kissed it. A contented moment that should have been played out in the privacy of a bedroom but out here under the stars somehow seemed equally intimate. They knew they were alone and today's events had taught them to live in the moment in case it was their last; a feeling Kaja wished she'd be able to hold onto and carry back to real life.

She let out a wistful sigh and laid her head on his bare shoulder. Right now a simple life seemed very appealing. One where all she needed was a naked Seth and somewhere to rest their heads. 'How long do you think we'll be out here before someone comes to find us?'

'Hopefully a while longer.' One suggestive look was all it took for Kaja's body to wake again in anticipation of more mind-blowing, bone-melting sex with him.

He tangled his fingers in her hair and pulled her in for a long, sensual kiss reaching every nerve-ending in her body. She put up no resistance when he lowered her back onto the ground and showed her what it was he intended to do with the extra alone time.

There were some aftershocks through the night but they gradually decreased in intensity. Kaja was certain they weren't the only ones sleeping outside when most residents would be afraid of staying indoors tonight in case of further structural damage. Although she was sure she was the only one waking up with a smile on her face. She knew there would be a fallout back in the city. Not only would they have to deal with repairs and casualties and generally getting the country back on its feet, but their loved ones would take precedence over examining what was happening between her and Seth. For now she was content to remain where she was.

As the sun rose, the sky around them changed from the inky black they'd fallen asleep under, to a warming *ombre* of pinks and golds, the beauty only eclipsed by the sight of the man she woke up to. His dark stubble combined with his mop of unruly hair gave him a wild look in keeping with the animal passion he'd unleashed.

She shivered with memories of what had kept them awake most of the night.

'Are you cold?' he mumbled, still half asleep, misunderstanding the trembling in her limbs. He pulled her closer to his chest and threw his leg over hers to share his body heat.

The movement brought them into contact in the most intimate of places so she could feel his body waking to start the new day. His burgeoning erection pressing against her was the early morning wake-up call she missed. Making love with Seth was something she'd never tire of or take for granted when she'd been without him in her bed for so long.

Kaja shifted position until he was sheathed inside her and hooked her legs around him as he drove deep into her core. This was the only place she wanted to be right now. The only place she wanted Seth. Worrying about everything else could wait until they could do something about it.

Once the sun had fully risen and the morning had well and truly begun it felt too indulgent, as well as risky, to continue lying au naturel in the open countryside. With the last of the water drained and every breadcrumb consumed they hadn't enough sustenance to keep on with their energetic sensual reunion. Well, her mind was willing but her body needed a rest before they resumed relations again. Something she was looking forward to after a proper meal and, preferably, in a comfortable bed.

They got dressed in yesterday's dirty, torn

clothes. Going home in these was the ultimate walk of shame although she hoped no one would guess what she had actually been doing all night. If the clothes didn't give her away the great big smile on her face might. Then she looked at the scene of utter devastation on top of the hill and quickly quashed the smug feeling. Residents had a lot more to worry about than her love life today. What was more, there would be a lot of people concerned about what had happened to her during the earthquake.

'Everything okay?' Seth glanced over at her as he pulled on his shoes and began tying his laces. 'You're very quiet.'

'I'm just wondering what we'll be going back to.' She was surprised to find her lip beginning to wobble as she spoke, the enormity of yesterday's events in full force now they would have to face the aftermath.

He shifted over beside her and helped her put her scrub top on, scooping her hair from inside the neckline to let it fall onto her shoulders. She leaned against him, gaining strength from simply having him taking care of her in such a small way. 'Whatever it is we'll face it together.'

'Will we, or are we just fooling ourselves, Seth? As much as I want a relationship to be possible, sleeping together won't magically make our problems disappear.'

'No, but it's a starting point. If we decide that's what we both want, surely we can work to make it happen?'

'It'll mean big changes for all of us.'

'Something I would be prepared to make as long as I know you're in it for the long haul this time.' He wasn't making a jibe at her; she could see he was being totally serious and with good reason. The last time he'd been planning a future with her she'd taken off and left him to pick up the pieces. Kaja knew she'd made the wrong decision at the time but there was one thing she was still holding back from Seth that could affect them as a couple. She was hesitant to make that promise to him now without being completely honest with him. In doing that there was a chance he wouldn't want to be with her at all and she wasn't ready to end things before they'd really begun.

'It's a big decision for me to make. Not because I don't want to be with you but there's a lot of stuff I would have to sort out before that could happen.' She knew it wasn't the answer he wanted but it was all she could give him for now.

He studied her quietly for a moment then said, 'I'll wait.'

It was such a comfort knowing he intended to stay by her side until she dealt with the issue that could end their relationship once and for all. She hadn't had that level of understanding for a long time, not since the day she'd left England. Now it was down to her to decide the next move.

In the distance she thought she heard the sound of a car out on the road. 'Seth, is that—'

He was already on his feet and running towards the first sign that they weren't out here alone. Kaja should've been elated but a heavy cloak of sadness settled around her shoulders, preventing her from getting up to follow. Once they left this place the fantasy was over and a selfish part of her wanted it to last for ever. The part of her who'd had this happy life with him once and thrown it all away. Only now did she truly realise how stupid she'd been.

'It's a police car,' he yelled back, jumping up and down trying to attract its attention.

'Great.' Kaja had to psych herself up to go and join him rather than lying down and praying she'd remain undiscovered.

If this was someone come to rescue them it was time to put her game face on. They were no longer two lovers stranded together enjoying some quality time, but a princess and her father's transplant surgeon, who'd been displaced during the country's worst earthquake in living history.

She could see the flashing lights on the car roof as it pulled into the car park and her stomach rolled at the prospect of being recognised in her current state or, worse, having to explain it. Without a mirror she didn't even know how bad she looked but she was guessing a day rescuing people trapped in the rubble of an earthquake and a night sleeping rough weren't going to make a pretty picture.

When she attempted to put her shoes on again it became apparent the swelling around her ankle would make that impossible. She had to limp barefoot towards the approaching police vehicle but held her head high, attempting to maintain some modicum of decorum.

Seth was leaning in through the open window

of the car when she got there, shaking hands with the officer in the driver's seat.

'Kaja, this is Constable Bailey, the white knight riding to our rescue.'

She winced at the casual use of her name, which suggested an intimacy between them that, while true, was no business of this complete stranger or those he would later retell his tale to.

'Good morning. Thank you for coming.' She was always self-conscious meeting new people but she had more reason than usual to worry about being judged. Especially when the young officer was openly gawping at her. Too late, she wondered if she had any grass stuck in her hair after rolling about in a field with Seth for most of last night.

'Oh, my goodness... I didn't realise...we were so busy with calls last night...they just said there were people stuck out at Tobel. No one said it was you!' He got out of the car and opened the door to the back seat, giving a little bow as he did so.

He hadn't known who he was coming to rescue. Whether he'd recognised her immediately or only when Seth had tossed her name into the conversation wasn't clear, but he knew who she was now and that was what mattered. It was important for her to try and claw back some respectability when she was at her most vulnerable.

'I'm sure you had more pressing matters to deal with last night. If you'd be kind enough to take us to the Royal Alderisi hospital we'd be very grateful. Mr Davenport, perhaps you'd like to ride up front with Constable Bailey here.' She wanted to reduce the chance of further impropriety to gossip about by separating them but if Seth's glower was anything to go by he wasn't impressed by the idea.

'Of course, Your Highness. I know my place.'

Kaja had hoped he'd understand her need to keep up a front even in these circumstances, but as he gave her a mock bow and jumped in the passenger seat she realised she was asking too much. Even more so when they were all settled in the car and he put in a request to their driver.

'If you don't mind, could you drop me off at the palace first? My daughter is there. She's all I have in the world and I want to make sure she's safe.' Seth's words cut deep. She understood his need to see his daughter as she also wanted to check on the welfare of her own family, but he was making it clear to her that things said or implied last night had simply happened in the heat of the moment. She was no more a priority in his world than she had been yesterday.

'Sure.'

'Do you know how the hospital and the palace fared in the earthquake?' Kaja kept her voice measured although her heart was cracking open, those old wounds she believed healed now ripping apart the old scar tissue.

The police officer spoke to her in the rear-view mirror. 'Yes, ma'am. The palace, as far as I know, wasn't too badly affected. All hospitals, as you'd imagine, are busy with the casualties, although no fatalities reported so far.'

'Thank goodness.' Despite all the reassurances she'd given herself and Seth, she exhaled all her fears for her loved ones in a long breath with the confirmation. She could see some of the tension released in Seth's shoulders in the passenger seat though he remained facing away from her.

'What about the people who reported our location? There was a man with serious crush injuries. Do you know anything about his condition?' Seth kept the questions coming and while Kaja genuinely wanted a progress report on the family she was glad it was keeping the focus off what they had been doing all the way out here in the first place.

'Sorry, I don't know. I just got the call to do a welfare check. I'm sure if they'd known it was you they would've had someone out here sooner.' He was twisting in his seat to apologise face to face but Kaja didn't want to risk an accident on her behalf.

'It's fine. We can make some enquiries when we get to the hospital. I'm sure Mr Davenport can use his influence to get that sort of information.'

'Oh, I don't know. I think Princess Kaja is pretty good at getting what she wants out of people.'

Officer Bailey glanced at each of them in turn. Seth wasn't exactly being discreet and neither was the heat steadily rising in her face. The atmosphere in the car was almost more unbearable than the one in the aftermath of the earthquake. She and Seth needed to talk, clear the air and lay down some ground rules. He couldn't play around with her reputation like this. That was, if they were going to have any relationship at all. At the moment the vibe he was giving her certainly wasn't all hearts and flowers.

'We're nearly at the palace. Perhaps I should get out here with you, Mr Davenport, and check things are all right at home?'

He met her gaze in the mirror with a steely glare of his own. 'No, I don't think that's a good idea. You should go on to the hospital. After all, you've sustained an injury and I don't think I'd be very popular if I prevented the country's princess from getting the necessary treatment.'

She couldn't swear to it but she thought the young constable put his foot down on the accelerator when he heard that. Kaja knew there was no point in arguing that it was not likely to be anything more than a sprained ankle when Seth would come back with some other smart answer. He wanted to be with his family and that didn't include her. She got the message loud and clear.

Kaja slumped back into the seat. There was no point arguing. It wasn't going to make her feel any better, only push Seth further away. If that were possible.

As they drove through the city, the car bumping around craters in the road, the sight of now derelict buildings spouting pillars of smoke and fire made her chest ache for all those affected. The desolate wasteland replacing the once vibrant country was an accurate depiction of her emotions over the past twenty-four hours.

Last night she'd been on top of the world thinking this was the beginning of a new life together for her and Seth. Now they were back to the real world where she didn't have him by her side.

She watched as the residents of the worst-affected houses set to work outside, banding together to clear away debris and salvage what was left of their lives here. If there was one thing she and the inhabitants had in common it was that survivor spirit. That ability to pick oneself up and get on with things though you'd lost everything dear to you was something she'd mastered. At least, she was good at pretending she had.

When Seth got out of the car and slammed

the door she knew what they'd had was over before it really began again. So why did it hurt so much more this time around?

CHAPTER ELEVEN

SETH STORMED UP to the house gates. If he'd been thinking clearly he would've let Kaja come on up as she'd suggested so he wouldn't have to go through the security rigmarole.

'I need some ID,' today's sentry demanded.

He flashed his hospital pass. 'You know who I am. You've seen me often enough. Now can you please let me in so I can see my daughter?'

The guard waved him through and Seth uttered a begrudging thanks.

This was typical of the nonsense in Kaja's world and he was sick of being reminded he wasn't part of it. Even in emergency situations they couldn't give him a break. Regardless of the fact that he'd probably saved the grand duke's life, he was never going to be accepted as Kaja's equal. She'd made that very point herself when she'd segregated herself in the back seat of the police car from the lesser mortals.

He hadn't come out here with the intention of

getting back together with Kaja but it had happened last night and it had been glorious. What he hadn't been prepared for was the fallout of being rejected again.

There had been no class distinction lying out there naked entwined in one another's arms. They had just been two people who'd needed each other. That had changed the second they'd been in the public domain and she'd acted embarrassed to be seen with him, reminding him once again that their lives weren't compatible and she could turn her back on him at any given moment.

The only person he should be concentrating on spending time with was his daughter. Especially as he hadn't been there at a time when she'd needed him most.

The interior of the palace remained relatively the same. It did look a tad more minimalist than he recalled, devoid of a few of the ornate—and perhaps fragile—furnishings. It wasn't immediately obvious if they'd been broken during the earthquake or hurriedly stored away but the place had been cleaned and tidied back to its original state. He could only guess by the absence of the huge chandelier in the hallway that they hadn't got away totally unscathed. Things could be replaced, loved ones couldn't. So when Amy came running at him he had to stifle a tear or two of relief.

'Am I glad to see you.' He crouched down so she ran straight into his arms and hugged her as tight as he could.

'Daddy, you're squishing me.' She pushed him off, then came back for a second, less squishy hug.

'Are you okay? Were you hurt?' He brushed her curls away from her face, checking for any signs of injury.

'It was scary, Daddy. The noise made me cry.' Her bottom lip trembled and Seth could feel his going too. He'd been afraid so he could only imagine what had gone on in her head in a strange place, so far from home without her father.

'I know, sweetheart. I'm so sorry I couldn't make it back to you.'

'She is fine. This was the safest place for her. A little noise, some shaking, but no one hurt. What about the princess? She is not with you?' Fatima was frowning at him as she wiped her hands on the apron tied at her waist. The thought that they might have been baking again made his stomach growl and remind him he hadn't had anything to eat other than the picnic leftovers last night.

'Thank you for taking care of Amy. I took Kaja out for a walk to clear her head after seeing her father at the hospital. I didn't know we'd get stuck out there all night. She's gone back to the hospital to check in with him.' Something he'd be sure to do too once he'd spent some time with Amy. As well as whatever upheaval had been caused by the earthquake at the hospital, they'd need a progress report on the grand duke's recovery post-surgery. There was a good chance of Bruno getting released today too if he hadn't had any complications overnight.

'I hear on the news the hospital is very busy. A lot of people hurt yesterday. We were all very lucky.' Fatima crossed herself and thanked the heavens they had all survived the experience.

'I should probably head down there too and see if I can be of any assistance.' It would be all hands on deck in the emergency department to get through the wave of casualties coming in.

They probably didn't have the staff numbers available with this kind of nationwide incident.

'You can do that after you have a shower and I make you something to eat.' Fatima steered him towards the staircase but it seemed selfish to be thinking only of himself during a crisis.

'I don't really have time—'

'Nonsense. You will be no use to anyone if you die of hunger first. Go, get washed and changed. I'll cook.' Fatima wasn't going to take no for an answer.

'Yeah, Daddy, you stink.'

'Charming,' he mumbled as he trudged up the stairs, dejected and rejected all at once.

'If you are going to be seen with the princess you really need to look the part. You don't want to shame her.' Fatima wasn't to know Kaja was equally grimy and unkempt but he supposed that would only earn her some fans to be seen mucking in with the rest of the community.

'No, Fatima, I would never want to shame her.' He would never do anything intentional to hurt her. That was why it was so galling when she could be so cruel to him without seeming to give it a second thought.

* * *

As expected, the hospital was a hub of activity. There were people, staff and beds everywhere as Seth walked in—unimpeded this time, although he was sure there were still guards posted outside the royal hospital rooms.

'Seth Davenport. I'm a surgeon. Can I do anything to help?' He'd been directed towards the co-ordinator in Reception, which was now serving as a triage area.

'We need all the help we can get. It's mostly stitches and broken limbs in here. The seriously injured were seen to first. You should have been here last night.' She snorted a humourless laugh as she handed him a stack of files before calling her next patient.

Seth could tell from her stained uniform and the bags under her eyes that she'd been here long past the end of her usual shift. 'Sorry, I was…stuck out at Tobel.'

She stopped shuffling files long enough to stare at him. 'You weren't the one who saved that family out there, were you?'

He wasn't sure he deserved praise next to someone who'd probably been on her feet since yesterday. 'I didn't do it alone and I'm sure the staff here did more than we did at the scene.'

'I was here when they came in. That straw trick was a stroke of genius for the punctured lung. The father's on the ward now if you want to go and see him?' It was a magnanimous offer when she was clearly under a lot of pressure to attend to the waiting patients but Seth was keen to see for himself how the man was doing.

'Would you mind? I swear I won't be long, then I'll come back here and get stuck into these.'

She held out her arms for him to offload the patient files. 'Don't worry, they'll still be here when you get back.'

Seth thought he'd take a quick look at the man's notes, maybe have a word with whoever was treating him, then he'd come back and set to work on that waiting list in the emergency department.

He hadn't counted on running into Kaja visiting at the same time.

'Hello. I wasn't expecting to see you here.' He should have been. She was always going to check up on a patient as well as setting to work to help everyone else who needed it. It was a foregone conclusion they were going to meet up at some point in the same building.

He hovered at the doorway, uncertain if he was going to stick around now when relations between them had turned sour.

'I just ducked in to see how he was doing while I was in between patients. He had emergency surgery when he came in but he's sleeping it off now. The surgeon said he'll recover. In time.'

'Good. What about the others?'

'Mum and daughter were a bit shaken up but they're okay.'

'And you? How's the ankle?' They were acting like strangers or, at most, colleagues with a patient in common, but it was safer than tackling what was really on his mind when it would only bring more pain.

Kaja lifted the bottom of her trouser leg up to show off a fresh bandage and an unattractive white clog. 'I think being seen in these shoes is more painful than the sprain. They could probably do with a little bling and more of a heel to fit in with the rest of my wardrobe.'

'They're not very you,' he agreed with a smirk. She was definitely more at home here in the midst of this organised chaos with barely enough time to breathe never mind care what she looked like, than swanning about in a palace.

'I shouldn't complain. The staff were very kind to lend me a change of clothes and patch me up. This is nothing compared to some of the injuries that have come in through the doors.'

'Speaking of which, I said I wouldn't be long. I promised to help out with the walking wounded.'

'Me too. I'll walk down with you.'

They left their sleeping patient and tiptoed out of the door. Well, Seth tiptoed. Kaja kind of squeaked across the floor.

'Did you manage to get anything to eat? Fatima wouldn't let me leave until my stomach was fit to burst.'

'Some of the locals have been fuelling us with coffee and cake. I'm glad Fatima made you take a break. You worked so hard yesterday; you deserve a rest.'

He didn't miss the coy look and guessed her mind had wandered to their energetic relations last night, and this morning, as well as the physical labour they'd put into rescuing the family. The way his had.

She cleared her throat. 'I see you had a chance to clean up as well. You look good.'

In trying to avoid using the elevator in case of any further power outages, they'd taken the stairs. It was the one relatively quiet area in the hospital but it also seemed to amplify their awkwardness around each other, along with their voices. Seth decided to address what had happened this morning rather than ignore it and let it fester. There was nothing worse than drifting apart from someone without having a chance to understand what had gone wrong.

He waited until they were halfway down, pausing on a landing to broach the subject. 'Kaja, are you ashamed of me?'

'What? No. Whatever gave you that idea?' Her frown gave the impression she was being honest with him but with evidence to the contrary he couldn't be certain.

'After last night I was willing to give things a shot. To the point of setting my ego aside until you decide if I'm enough for you. Then the policeman turned up and you went cold on me, making sure I sat up front with the other "civilian".'

'Seth, it wasn't like that at all. I don't know, I panicked when he recognised me and I was worried he'd guess what had happened between us. I don't want people gossiping and speculating before we even figure out what's going on between us. Last night was special. I'm certainly not ashamed about what happened.' She rested her hand lightly on his arm, imploring him with those big eyes to believe her.

'Nor me, but I need to know where I stand. I'm not going to set myself up for another fall, Kaja. Not when I've got Amy to consider in all of this too. If we're going to make a go of things we both have to be on board one hundred per cent. I'm not convinced you're ever going to be.'

'That's not fair, Seth.'

'I'm being honest. Something I think you need to be with yourself too.' He was no longer willing to leave room for confusion. It was all or nothing; he wasn't going to risk his heart again.

The silence as Kaja contemplated what he was saying went on for an eternity before she broke it. 'I've been thinking about that and I would like to go back to medicine.'

'So what are you going to do about it, Kaja?'

'Pardon?'

'There's nothing to be gained by simply thinking how you could improve your life here. You have to actually do something to make it happen and fight for what's important to you. What is it you want, Kaja?' It had to come from the heart if she was going to be honest with herself and him.

'I want… I want…'

'What?'

'I want the life I had in England.' She blurted it out, surprising them both, judging by the shocked look on her face. Seth had no intention of leaving it there.

'Why, when you gave it up to come back here?'

'Because I was leading my own life. I had a job I loved and…and… I had you, Seth.' When her voice cracked he had to swallow down the urge to hold her and comfort her. This was make or break for him.

'Five years ago you didn't want any of that.'

'I did, I swear, but I thought I had to give it all up because none of it was real.'

'What's changed now?'

'I'm miserable here, Seth,' she sobbed. 'I came back to do the right thing by my family but it cost me everything. Being with you last night was the first time in a long time that I was actually happy. I want that to last.'

'So, I'll ask you again. What are you going to do about it?' He rested his hands on her shoulders, resisting the full-on embrace he wanted to give her.

'I'm going to speak to my father about stepping down from my royal duties. I'll tell him I want to go back to medicine full time. I don't know how we're going to do it yet but I also want a life with you, Seth. If that's what you'd like too?' She looked up at him, so full of hope, his heart soared. Everything was out in the open now. No more secrets preventing them from forging ahead. She wouldn't have the conversation with her father if she wasn't serious about making the changes it would take for him to risk his heart on her again. It was his turn to take a leap of faith and prove his commitment to their relationship by forgiving her for her earlier slight.

'It's all I could ever ask for.' They could work out the logistics later. For now it was all the confirmation he needed to go with his heart.

He leaned in and laid his mouth gently upon hers just to experience that connection once more until they had a chance to get some quality time alone again.

'So, we're good?' Kaja broke away to check but Seth didn't want to stop kissing her now that the obstacles to true love had apparently been removed.

'We're good.' He smiled against her lips. Just one more kiss and he'd get back to work.

They heard the squeak of a door being opened at the top of the stairs and he remembered to cool it. Kaja was right, they didn't need to have their every move analysed or have bystanders commenting on what they thought of their relationship. They had to figure things out for themselves.

'Can we pick this up again later?'

'Just give me the word and I'll come a-calling.'

That demure, lowered-lashes look she was

giving him, unaware of how completely under her thrall he was, would ensure he came back time and time again.

'You are such a dork.' She slapped him on the arm, her laughter every bit as intoxicating as her kisses.

'You're such a princess,' he teased back, and to the female visitor coming down the stairs behind them they probably looked like two friends engaging in a bit of banter, which was exactly what they wanted people to think.

Now he understood her need to protect their relationship he wasn't going to take it personally. This way it kept Amy out of the spotlight too. It would be such a change in their family dynamic for him to have a partner it was something he'd have to lead into gradually with her. She didn't need to see their faces splashed all over the newspapers with the gossip columns listing all the reasons this single, divorced dad wasn't a good match for the country's princess. He didn't need reminding when he felt it so acutely every time he looked at her.

He bounded down the remainder of the steps, much lighter for having set the record straight with Kaja and with something to look forward to at the end of his shift.

They worked on into the night assisting where they could, patching people up so they were able to go home as soon as possible. Occasionally Kaja caught sight of Seth behind a cubicle curtain or walking by with his next patient as she treated hers.

After their talk on the stairs she hoped this was the start of a new life together for them. But there was still something she'd kept from him and if they were going into this with a clean slate she knew she'd have to tell him about her infertility issues. Her stomach tied itself in knots every time she thought about the last time she'd told a man she couldn't have his child, but Seth was nothing like Benedikt. Hurting anyone on purpose simply wasn't in his nature.

She could hear him now, his deep voice soothing the screams of a small child obviously in pain.

'I know it hurts, Lottie, but I need you to keep still so I can take a good look at that eye.

Mrs Gallo, perhaps you could help hold your daughter still for me.'

Kaja had a few minutes to spare and small children were never the easiest patients to wrangle. Perhaps she could provide a suitable distraction for the little girl to enable Seth to do what he had to.

'Hey. Sorry for disturbing you, Mr Davenport. I'm in between patients at the minute and wondered if there was anything I could do to help?' There was a fine line between offering assistance and being seen as interfering.

If anything, he seemed relieved to see her.

'Thank you. I think Lottie here might need a little more persuading to sit still for me.'

Her mother was trying to stop her from rubbing her already red eyes with her bunched-up fists.

'Did you get something in your eye, Lottie? They must be very sore.' Kaja took a seat at the side of the bed as the little girl nodded and sniffed.

'I think she might have some grit irritating her. We need to get some fluorescein stain in to check.' He was as reassuring to an infant with a sore eye as he was to a fully grown woman trapped under rubble. It didn't matter what background he came from, Seth's caring and understanding nature was the mark of a true gentleman. He was pure class as far as she was concerned. A prince amongst men.

'The doctor needs to see what's hurting you, Lottie. We need you to keep your eye wide open so he can do that. Do you think you could be a big girl and tilt your head back for me?' There was no more reason to trust her than the handsome man trying to help her, but Kaja was hoping that by teaming up they would manage to persuade her.

If there was something stuck to the cornea it would explain the red, watery reaction. It could also be something more serious, such as a piece of metal. That could require surgery.

Kaja gently eased the girl's hands away from her eyes. Although Lottie let her, she did let out a pitiful whine and tensed her whole body.

'I couldn't see anything in there but I did try to give her an eye bath with some hot water. It didn't help.' The mother fretted from the other side of the bed as she brushed her daughter's hair away from her forehead.

'That's fine. We advise people not to try and

remove any foreign bodies from the eye themselves in case they do further damage. You were right to bring her to us.' Seth's assurance she'd done her best eased the anxious look on the woman's face.

Kaja stood up alongside Seth so the child was looking up at her, keeping her hands tightly in hers so she wouldn't suddenly lash out. 'You just keep watching me, Lottie, while Mr Davenport takes a look in your eye.'

Seth held her eyelids open so he could have a look and the little girl squeezed Kaja's hand.

'I can't see anything in there so we're going to have to use the dye.' He clearly didn't want to distress her any more than necessary but if there was something irritating her it could cause conjunctivitis or lead to scarring.

'Lottie, the doctor is going to touch your eye with a small piece of paper. You just keep looking up at me, okay?' Another hand squeeze and whimper in response.

'I need you to blink on this for me, Lottie,' Seth coaxed, then addressed her mother to explain the process. 'The blotting paper contains an orange dye, which, when used in conjunction with a blue light, detects any foreign bodies or damage to the cornea. Blinking helps spreads the dye.'

He did the test as quickly as his patient would allow then whisked the paper away again.

'You're so good, Lottie. Now I'm going to shine a torch on you. There's nothing to be afraid of. It's a very special torch.' Seth turned the torch on so she could see the light for herself, shining it on her hand then on the ceiling so she could see it wasn't harmful.

'Is it magic?' Lottie was captivated now, the tears giving way to childish curiosity.

'Well, hopefully this will help us make you feel better again. Just keep your eye open for us, Lottie.' It was down to Kaja again to reassure her while Seth inspected the site. Any problems on the cornea would show up green under the blue light.

He had to look under the eyelid first, causing Lottie to tense up again. 'Okay… I think I can see something on the surface. I'm going to put some special eye drops in to stop it hurting, Lottie.'

It was difficult to make sure she didn't blink out the local anaesthetic drops but Seth persevered.

'I'm sure we'll have people of all ages coming in with the same problem given the air quality after the earthquake. It will be full of dust.' Kaja kept talking as Seth used a cotton swab to remove the grit.

Every adult in the room breathed a sigh of relief and when no one else was looking, he gave Kaja a wink. Confirmation if it was needed that they made a good team.

'All done. I'll put a dressing over that eye just to make it more comfortable for a day or two. Try not to rub your eye if you can help it, Lottie. It shouldn't give you any more trouble but if it does Mum should make an appointment with your GP to get it checked out.'

'Thank you, Doctor.' Mrs Gallo waited until he'd taped a dressing over the eye before enthusiastically shaking his hand. Then she bent down and gave her daughter a kiss on the top of the head before they disappeared out of the cubicle, leaving Seth and Kaja alone.

'I'm glad we didn't have to refer her to the surgical team to cause any more trauma. Thanks for the moral support too. I'm sure it would've taken me twice as long if you hadn't been here.'

'It's never easy with the young ones and

nearly always a two-person job. It's not the easiest task to perform either. I presume you've done that a few times to take on the job yourself?'

'Once or twice during hospital placements. You weren't so bad yourself, with the kiddie-whispering. She was putty in your hands once you gave her some attention, much like Amy. It seems no one is immune to the princess's charms. At least, no one under the age of six.' Beyond the complimenting was that teasing that made her blush and bluster at the same time.

'Then your daughter is a good judge of character, even if her father's opinion of me wavers from time to time.' She wasn't going to let him completely off the hook about earlier. Although she hoped she'd put his mind at rest by telling him about her plans. It wasn't going to be an easy conversation with her father, but one that was overdue.

'My opinion on you is rock solid.' He wrapped his arms around her waist before gently fitting his lips expertly around hers. Seth was the tonic she needed for her increasing tiredness but it couldn't last when there were more patients piling in by the moment.

'The next shift is here to take over.' Seth poked his head into the cubicle to notify her that it was the end of their working day.

'I'm just finishing up in here and I'll be with you in a minute.' She'd been so busy she hadn't had time to think about taking a break but every part of her poor body was aching.

Resisting the urge to leave with him there and then, she turned back to the young man sitting on the bed with his hand in a cast. 'If you make an appointment out at Reception for the fracture clinic, we'll see how your fingers are healing in a few weeks' time.'

'Okay, thank you, Doctor.'

Even though most of the people through the door had recognised her at some stage, or had been made aware of her identity, once they were in their doctor/patient roles it didn't seem to matter. She preferred it that way, being accepted and respected for her medical expertise rather than her family background. It gave her a sense of purpose and, if she was honest, more self-respect to be of some use to her country rather than merely tabloid fodder.

The earthquake had put life into perspective for a lot of people and most of those affected were only too glad to have an extra pair of doctor hands available to care about who she was outside the hospital doors.

With her last patient discharged she went straight to find Seth. 'I could get used to this freedom, you know.'

He looked at the people still waiting to be seen in the reception area. 'I'm not sure your colleagues would be keen to be so "free" every day.'

'You know what I mean. Haven't you noticed?' She leaned in to whisper in case saying it aloud would somehow jinx it all. 'No bodyguards shadowing my every move.'

It brought Seth up short and she could see him checking for any ninja-like security hiding in the shadows, waiting to pounce. 'What happened to them?'

'I told them they weren't needed. They weren't around yesterday when my personal security was threatened and I survived. I couldn't very well work efficiently in the midst of the emergency here with them getting in the way or vetting every single person I came into contact with.' That conversation with Gunnar had been the first step in reasserting herself. She had a long way to go, decisions to make and conversations to have, but Seth had shown her she should be enjoying her life, not simply existing.

'Good for you. If I'm not careful your father will have me thrown out of the country for being a bad influence on you.' He laughed but Kaja suspected there was a smidgen of real concern mixed in there too.

'Don't worry, Papa is well aware I know my own mind.' She knew he was still groggy when he'd agreed to get security to back off but he was the same man who'd given into her desire to leave the country and study in England all those years ago. That hadn't been down to anyone's influence other than her own, even if Seth had been the main reason for her extended stay.

'I think you've proved your medical worth here today, if that was ever in doubt. You are so much more than a pretty princess, Kaja, and it's time the rest of the world knew that too.'

Kaja could virtually feel her skin smouldering under his intense gaze. They had to get out of here if they intended to keep their love life under wraps. Eye-sexing each other in the middle of a busy hospital wasn't being discreet.

'I…er…mightn't have given up all of my royal privileges. I hope you won't think any less of me but I've texted for the chauffeur to come and pick me up.'

One step at a time. Perhaps some day she'd start driving herself but not all changes were going to happen overnight.

He didn't say anything as they left the reception area and she braced herself for criticism about her sense of entitlement or, at the very least, a look of disapproval. Instead, he turned to her once they were outside and simply said, 'Thank goodness. I don't think I could walk after the past twenty-four hours and I'm not the one with a dodgy ankle.'

She wanted to kiss this man and, in keeping with her new vow to be true to herself, she did just that. Albeit at the side of the entrance where there was no lighting or prying eyes. Small steps. Big smooches.

When she saw the headlights approaching the front of the hospital instead of parking around the back with the normal visitors she had to let go of him again. At least he knew now it wasn't a rejection of him but of those around them knowing their business. When they were ensconced in the back seat of the car, Seth reached for her hand and she took it gladly. With him in her corner she knew she could make it through whatever challenges were thrown at her. In her uncertain world she was sure of one thing. Her love for Seth Davenport.

CHAPTER TWELVE

'NEXT TIME YOU go walkabout in the middle of an earthquake give me a heads up, will you?' Bruno lit in on Kaja as soon as she walked in through the door, but his tentative hug said he was more pleased to see her than angry at her.

'I can't promise you anything but I am sorry I didn't get to see you before you were discharged.' He looked so good considering he'd just had surgery the day before, better than she did after a long day on the front line of emergency medicine.

He shook hands with Seth. 'No worries. I think you had more important things to deal with. Good to see you again, too. Thanks for keeping an eye on my little sis yesterday. I knew we didn't have to worry too much if she was with you and since you both disappeared at the same time…'

Her brother wasn't stupid. There was no way he could know exactly what they'd got up to but the wink he gave them implied he was aware something was going on between them. Thankfully he was too polite to ask them outright.

'Daddy!' Amy made a flying leap at her father, confident he would catch her. Which he did, holding onto her legs as she wrapped them around his waist and hung her arms around his neck. She was always so overjoyed to see him Kaja was almost moved to tears. The way Seth hugged and made such a fuss of Amy his love for her was unquestionable. She tried to ignore that tug on her heart telling her she would never have that bond with a child of her own so it wouldn't spoil the moment.

'Oh, Miss Kaja, you're so filthy.' Fatima scuttled over, hands up in horror as she took in the spectacle of her working clothes. An unknown concept in the Alderisi family wardrobe.

'I did get stuck out there during an earthquake.' She laughed to cover her embarrassment when everyone else was so clean and tidy in comparison. Thank goodness she'd had at least one change of clothes since yesterday.

'I know, I know, Mr Davenport told me. You're so brave and compassionate to go and help those people without thinking about yourself.'

'I don't know about that.' Kaja shied away from the praise. It was circumstance and a desire to be useful that had driven her to act.

'What other princess would do that? Tell me. Who?' Fatima demanded from Bruno and Seth and they were stumped to come up with an answer. Which, it turned out, was the correct response. 'See? Only Miss Kaja.'

'Seth was there too—'

'Yes, and when he came home I made him shower and eat too.' She took Kaja's hand and tugged her towards the staircase.

'I wouldn't try arguing if I was you.' Seth was openly laughing at her as he swung Amy around so she was hoisted on his hip.

Not even her brother was in her corner. 'We've all had the same treatment. It's your turn.'

She stuck her tongue out at him when Fatima wasn't looking, just as she had when they were kids. Like then, Bruno simply laughed it off.

'You need a nice relaxing bath. I could arrange a massage if you want?'

'That won't be necessary, thanks.' For a moment she truly believed Fatima was going to accompany her upstairs to bathe her. As much as she appreciated the concern Kaja drew the line at that.

'Well, you need to take it easy. And eat. I will make you something. Yes, I will make dinner for everyone.' Hands on hips, Fatima decreed that was what was going to happen. A sit-down, home-cooked meal.

'Thank you, Fatima. That would be lovely.' Kaja was exhausted, usually this sort of thing would prove even more draining, but as she looked around she realised there was no one else she'd rather be with tonight than the people around her right now. They weren't all blood relations but they certainly felt like family to her.

The bath had gone some way to helping her relax. She'd used some perfumed oils and lit some candles and the stresses of the day had begun to melt away. It was only her still-throbbing ankle, now an attractive purple and yellow hue, reminding her of yesterday's trauma.

She threw on Seth's old sweatshirt—freshly laundered—and her tracksuit bottoms so she could properly relax for the rest of the evening.

The sound of chatter and the smell of freshly baked bread led her down to the dining room. Amy darted out in front of her just outside the door, almost causing her to trip.

'Be careful, Amy, that floor can be slippery.'

'Okay, Kaja. I'm helping Fatima.'

'Good girl. Remember to walk, don't run. We don't want any accidents or you'll end up like me.' Kaja showed off her freshly bandaged ankle and watched as the excited child skipped off so full of self-importance at whatever task Fatima had assigned to keep her out of mischief.

She hadn't intended to eavesdrop but when she heard the men talking she couldn't bring herself to interrupt the conversation. It would be good for them to get to know each other better if Seth and Amy were going to prove a more permanent feature in her life.

'Amy's a real whirlwind. You're very lucky, Seth.' Bruno's voice rendered her immobile.

'I know. I couldn't imagine life without her.'

'And her mother? I haven't heard anybody mention her. Sorry if that's insensitive of me to ask.'

She could imagine Seth shaking his head

to ease her brother's conscience that he might have inadvertently offended him in some way. 'Paula left not long after Amy was born. We're divorced now.'

'Sorry to hear that. I'm looking forward to marrying Missy and having a family of my own one day. What about you? Do you think you'll ever do it again?'

'Absolutely. I'll make sure to pick the right woman next time. Joking aside though, I can't wait to settle down again and have more children. I adore being a dad.'

It took a while for the reality of Seth's words to sink in, Kaja's heart plummeting when she realised his plans for the future included an extended family she couldn't provide him. Her heart couldn't take disappointing him month after month.

Seth was a fantastic dad. It was clear in every second he spent with his daughter and even today when he'd treated that young girl so compassionately. It wouldn't be fair to deny him the chance of settling down with someone who could give him everything he wanted. More children and the chance to experience it all again. Amy would make a great big sister too.

It was Kaja who didn't fit into that picture-perfect happy family.

Just because she was forced to suffer a childless future it didn't mean he had to.

Seth was a good man who deserved better than a barren princess who would bring him nothing but pain. Perhaps they should stick to the original plan and let him go back home without her. She shouldn't expect him to disrupt the life he had with Amy for her sake. Not when she still couldn't be the woman he needed. Even if she gave up her royal title, her loyalties no longer divided, she was failing him in the most basic fashion. She'd been selfish in not telling him before now simply so she could have him in her life a little longer.

Ending things now had to be better than waiting until he resented her for not giving him a baby. She'd been there before with Benedikt and knew how this panned out: disappointment, accusing fingers and crying herself to sleep every time she didn't meet expectations.

'What are you doing out here? Food is on the table going cold. Go, join the others.' Fatima, closely followed by her little shadow, Amy, both carrying baskets of bread rolls, harried her into the dining room.

Seth and Bruno were pleased to see her and she didn't think it was merely so they could finally tuck into their dinner. It was unfortunate she was going to have to spoil the evening for one of them.

'Much better.' Seth approved of Kaja's new attire. It was funny how he found an old baggy sweatshirt on her just as attractive as the expensive couture she wore in public. Probably because it reminded him of the previous life they'd had. One he hoped they'd have again. This time with an alternative ending.

She flashed him a subtle smile and took a seat beside her brother on the opposite side of the table. Amy jumped up on the seat beside Seth, on the cushion they were using as a booster seat so she could see over the table. It was how he imagined a medieval banqueting table would look in terms of the amount of food and the length of the actual table, although the assortment of shining cutlery and obviously expensive china created an altogether more regal experience. He wasn't used to all this pomp and ceremony for dinner. Usually, if Amy had already been fed by the childminder, he settled for dinner on a tray in front of the TV.

'I was just telling Seth the hospital rumour mill was working overtime today.' Bruno poured Kaja a glass of wine so she could catch up with the one they'd already downed waiting for her.

'Oh?' Seth noticed the wary look in her eyes. She probably assumed the worst, the way he had when Bruno had mentioned it to him too, but she didn't need to worry. Their al fresco tryst remained a secret as far as he knew.

'Yes, you impressed quite a few with your dedication, pitching in with everybody else. I mean, I know you were there too, Seth, but people don't expect to see anyone from the royal family getting their hands dirty in the midst of a crisis.' Bruno was very matter-of-fact about the way his family was viewed by the public. Unlike his sister, he didn't seem to care a jot what other people thought of him.

It was always different for men, of course; they weren't judged as much as their female counterparts on their looks or their relationships. However, Seth got the impression Bruno wouldn't compromise his sense of self for anyone.

'It wasn't anything I hadn't done before. Just because you haven't been down at the coalface, big bro, doesn't mean I haven't.'

'Well, I heard you had to staple a man's scalp back together.'

'True.'

'And the kid impaled on the handlebars?'

'Also true.'

'What about the baby you single-handedly delivered in the back of the ambulance.'

'Not true. There were three of us.'

Seth scooped some of the pasta dish Fatima had made for them onto Amy's plate before serving himself while the siblings discussed some of the patient stories that had circulated about Kaja's time at the hospital. He devoured the cheesy, creamy comfort food as though he hadn't eaten all day. If he stayed here much longer letting Fatima fatten him up he might have to invest in some trousers with an elastic waist. Goodness knew how Kaja kept her svelte figure. Stress, he supposed. It was impossible to enjoy a hearty meal properly if your stomach was constantly in knots with worry.

Even now he noticed her picking at her dinner, not eating more than a forkful or two. He'd have a chat with her later to put her mind at ease that no one had mentioned the possibility of a romance between them in his presence. After Amy and the others went to bed he was looking forward to having some alone time again with Kaja. Libido aside, they needed to figure out how they were going to make this work between them. If she was as unhappy as she appeared here and so keen to get back to work, he hoped it wouldn't take too much to persuade her to return to England with him once her father was fully recovered.

'No more hospital talk, please. People are trying to eat.' After hearing one too many surgical procedures Fatima held her hands up to her ears, although she was the only one who seemed bothered. Amy was more concerned with getting a second helping of pasta than any hospital drama.

'Sorry, Fatima,' Kaja and Bruno chorused, sounding nothing of the sort. He could imagine the two of them as mischievous children running rings around her when she was the only one giving them any attention without their parents around.

'I told Dad what you'd been doing. He was very impressed.'

'I don't know why. I am a qualified surgeon. I worked in England for a long time in the emergency department and I do the same here once a week, as he very well knows.' Kaja stabbed her pasta.

'He's very old-fashioned when it comes to our roles. Perhaps it's different now he knows it's not some vanity project you're running. It could be that he's going through some sort of epiphany. After all, he's received a second chance at life.'

'Thanks to you.'

'Thanks to all of us. If it weren't for you, we wouldn't have got Seth here involved, and Fatima has been the one keeping us all going. Not to forget Amy, who is a ray of sunshine here and I'm sure will play a part in Dad's recovery.' Bruno held up his glass of wine. 'To us.'

'To us,' the rest of them toasted along with him. Including Amy with her beaker of milk.

Kaja set down her glass and her cutlery, abandoning any pretence she was eating. 'I've decided to go back to medicine full time.'

'That's a big deal, sis. There will be a lot of logistics to consider. People to consult.'

'I'm aware of that but I can serve the country better that way.' For the first time since bringing up the subject she looked at Seth.

'You're staying here?' He didn't care that no one else was aware there was a different option available to her if she chose. She did. He'd really believed this was going to be their second chance. If she was expecting him to fall into line with her decision and relocate here permanently, uprooting Amy from everything she knew, she really should've consulted him on the matter first.

'Yes.'

'Oh, Miss Kaja, you are a very honourable woman. Your mother would be so proud.' Fatima, close to tears at the news, rose from her seat and threw her arms around Kaja's neck in a hug. Bruno remained seated, his gaze travelling between her and Seth.

Seth couldn't move even if he wanted to.

'You're really going to give everything up

here for the stress and drama of an emergency department?'

'Give up what, Bruno? I don't have anything I'm not willing to drop to give my life some meaning.' She didn't look at Seth but every word was a thousand daggers plunging into his flesh. There were so many reasons for him to take offence in that one simple sentence. Apparently he was nothing.

That wasn't what she'd told him hours earlier when they were planning a future together. She'd told him she was giving up her position to do what she wanted in life. Now, suddenly he wasn't a part of that? If she'd changed her mind and decided he wasn't worth giving up her position for after all, there were kinder ways to do it. She could've broken it to him in private, for a start. There was no way she wouldn't have known how hurtful those words would be and she had to have a reason why she'd wanted to wound him so deeply. By doing this to him in company she was denying him the chance to call her out on those empty promises she'd made. Not that it mattered now, when the damage had already been done.

He was mad at himself for falling for her all

over again and believing her vow to speak to her father. She'd probably only said it to stop him hounding her when he'd been pushing her so hard to give him the answer he wanted to hear. Now she'd had time to think it through, a life with him wasn't any more attractive to her than it was five years ago.

'I think we should leave you to discuss family matters in private. Amy, it's bedtime.' Seth tossed his linen napkin on the table and pushed back his chair, desperate to escape the room and this conversation.

'I'm not tired, Daddy.' Amy folded her arms across her chest and pouted in an uncharacteristic bout of petulance at the worst possible time.

'It's getting late and I've had a very trying day. Let's go, Amy.' He was pleading with her in his head not to cause an even greater scene when he was already at breaking point. It wasn't his temper he was worried about losing, rather control of his fragile emotions. In the space of a few minutes his dreams of becoming a family with Kaja had been shattered, only to be faced with returning to his lonely life back in England. And he had no idea why.

Thankfully his daughter gave up on her sit-in and climbed down off her chair. 'Night, night, everybody.'

'Night, sweetheart.' Seth had to wait not so patiently while Kaja came to give her a hug, closely followed by Fatima.

He managed an abrupt, 'Goodnight,' before taking his daughter by the hand and leading her away from the family they'd both begun to feel a part of. Returning home was going to break both of their hearts.

There was no way he was sleeping until he confronted Kaja about her comments tonight. Once Amy had brushed her teeth and settled into bed he crept out onto the landing separating their apartments from Kaja's. He made sure to leave the doors open in case she stirred while he was waiting for answers.

When Kaja appeared he was sure he saw her take a deep breath as she met him at the top of the stairs.

'Do you mind telling me what that was all about down there?' He practically spat the words at her.

'I told you I'm going back into medicine permanently.'

'But you're staying here?'

'Where else would I work? This is my country. My family are here.'

'What about Amy and me? I thought we meant something to you.'

'You'll always have a special place in my heart, Seth. Amy too. But I've had some time to think and I want to focus on me and my career. I can't do that if I'm playing house with you and your daughter.' She was so calm and cool as she devastated him Seth thought it was worse than having her simply disappear from his life, seeing first-hand of how little significance he was to her.

'What's changed in the space of a few hours? Earlier we were making plans to get together again, then you dump me halfway through dinner. It doesn't make any sense.'

'We want different things. I heard you talking to Bruno, telling him your plans to get married and have more children. That's not going to happen with me.'

'That's what all of this is about? A snatched bit of small talk between me and your brother?'

He wanted to laugh at the absurdity of it. 'In an ideal world, yes, I'd like to settle down again. That's not so bad, is it?'

He moved towards her, wanted to hold her again so she could remember how it felt to be wrapped up in each other's arms and forget everything else.

Kaja stepped back, reluctant to let him touch her. 'What if I told you I can't have children, Seth? I can't give you that family you want. Would you still want to be with me?'

That bombshell rendered him speechless. It was such a huge thing for her to have kept from him all this time and he was trying to process what that meant for them. He'd pictured building on their family but now he had to adjust to the idea of a future without further children.

Unfortunately, Kaja took his pause as he processed this news as the rejection she'd been expecting.

'I'll take that as a no. Just as I thought.'

'That's not what—'

She rejected his attempt to placate her with a wave of her hand. 'Forget it, Seth. I've made up my mind.'

'And what? That's the end of it? No discussion?'

'Exactly. What's the point of pretending there's a future for us? My career is all I'm interested in now. It's the only thing I have going for me.'

'What am I supposed to do? Forget anything ever happened between us and carry on living here and treating your father?' It had been hard enough to do that first time around but now, with such new and erotic memories of their time together, it would be impossible. Not to mention painful, with the knowledge she wasn't going to fight for them this time either. It seemed Kaja was ready to walk away every time they faced an obstacle and that wasn't a stable foundation for any relationship. Perhaps she was right after all. This was never going to work between them.

'I wouldn't expect you to do that. That's why I think you and Amy should go home. You were flown in to do the transplant and you managed that successfully. We have a team of surgeons and consultants who can oversee the rest of his recovery. If there are any complications they can't handle I'm sure they'll be in touch.'

'You have it all figured out, don't you?' He wondered if this was the royal equivalent of ordering a taxi for a regrettable one-night stand the morning after. She couldn't wait to get rid of all traces of him.

'I don't see the point in dragging things out.'

'Thanks for being so honest with me. It makes a change.' He was lashing out now, wishing to cause her some of the pain she was currently causing him, but she didn't flinch. Only one day returned to her world and that cool princess was well and truly back in charge. When she offered no defence against his jibe he knew the battle was lost. She didn't even feel strongly enough to argue with him any more. He walked away defeated, knowing he wasn't wanted enough for anyone to fight to have him in their lives.

Kaja opened her bedroom curtains, the morning sunshine unreflective of her current disposition. She'd slept later than she'd intended. Mainly because it had taken her so long to get to sleep, her guilty conscience replaying her harsh words and the image of Seth's crestfallen face on a loop in her head. She knew she'd hurt him. Again. This time, she told herself, it was for his benefit, not hers. It was completely different.

Five years ago she'd run from their relationship, realising she couldn't make a lifelong commitment to him when she wasn't being true to herself. Now, she was saving him from doing the same. It didn't make her feel any better. He wanted to be with someone who could give him a family and he could pretend otherwise to be with her but they both knew it was the truth. Her body had failed her and the man she loved.

Unwilling to face anyone this morning, she made the decision to go straight to the hospital and assist where she could once she washed and dressed. There'd be time later for her to deal with her brother's questions, Fatima mourning the inevitable loss of her young companion and, worst of all, being faced with Seth's look of betrayal. Unfortunately, the pain in her own heart couldn't be avoided so easily. The best she could do was try and work through it.

CHAPTER THIRTEEN

'I'M GOING TO take a break and go and check on my father.'

'No problem. It's quietened down a bit for now. Thanks for your help. You've really gone above and beyond over these past few days.' Cecilia, the woman who'd been co-ordinating all available staff in the emergency department, threw her arms around Kaja and hugged her. It was unexpected on a number of different levels. Kaja hadn't been working here to garner praise of any kind, but she had enjoyed being seen as part of the team rather than simply for novelty value. Cecilia was hugging her as a colleague, perhaps even a friend, without thought to her royal status.

The simple gift of a hug had her too choked up to bat away the compliment or offer any response. Instead she gave her a squeeze back and walked away before she made a fool of herself bawling in the middle of the corridor.

Of course, when she came to her father's hospital room she had to erase all traces of that vulnerability. If she was asserting her right to work and step back from her royal duties it was necessary to show confidence in what she was doing.

'Kaja.' Her father struggled to sit up when she came in through the door.

'There's no need to strain yourself, Papa. I just wanted to see how you were today.' She walked over and kissed him before helping him into a more comfortable position. He had more colour in his cheeks today and appeared brighter than he had in months.

'Sore, but I'll live and that's the main thing.'

'Yes, it is.' It seemed he'd inherited her brother's dark sense of humour along with his kidney, but that wasn't altogether a bad thing. If he'd stopped taking everything so seriously it might make it easier for her to discuss her plans for the future without the dramatics she'd been expecting.

She pulled a chair over so she could sit by the side of his bed and took his hand in hers.

'Papa, I've been thinking a lot about my life and I'm not happy with where I am right now.

Some things have happened while you've been in here, which have made me reassess what I'm doing and what sort of legacy I'm leaving behind.' She mightn't be able to secure the royal line with children of her own, but she could make a difference by saving lives.

'It's about time.'

It certainly wasn't the response she'd anticipated. 'Pardon me?'

Her father rested his other hand on top of hers. 'Kaja, you haven't been happy since you came home from England. I had hoped marriage would give you something to focus on rather than whatever it was you'd left behind. I wanted you to have the love and happiness your mother and I shared. I'm sorry that didn't happen with Benedikt. What he did to you was unforgivable. I've been waiting so very long for you to find something to make you smile again.'

If she didn't have so many questions Kaja might have been stunned into silence. 'You don't mind if I go back into medicine full time? What about all your talk about family traditions and keeping up appearances?'

'All I ever wanted was for you to be happy,

my darling. Without your royal duties these past five years I was worried you wouldn't leave the house at all, you were so miserable.'

'You never said any of this before. I thought I was a disappointment.'

'Never. I know I may not have been the best father over the years, consumed by my responsibilities elsewhere, but I was always proud of you.'

'Why didn't you reach out to me when I was in England?'

'Your mother thought we should give you space and you'd come back to us when you were ready. You did. We both just wanted the best for you. Then you met Benedikt and I thought you were focusing on the future.'

'I tried, but apparently I never did get over my past,' she muttered more to herself than for her father's ears. She'd never loved anyone but Seth and in hindsight it must've been obvious to her ex that she was on the rebound and not fully committed to their marriage. Looking back now, she couldn't completely blame him for seeking affection elsewhere. He could've discussed it with her, of course, rather than humiliating her with his affair, but they'd been doomed from the start when she was still in love with another man.

'You seemed to over these past few days.'

She wasn't entirely sure what he meant by that when he didn't know a fraction of what had been going on outside this room, but he was right. With Seth back in her life she had been able to put a lot of their bad history behind her. Mainly because he'd forgiven her, but also because she was happier simply having him around. Both of which were moot points now that she'd hurt him all over again and told him she didn't want him in her life.

'Are you telling me that all the decisions I've made have been based on my own paranoia?'

'I can't say that. I don't know what goes on in your head but please understand I don't want anything to stop you living your best life. Do what makes you happy, not what you think other people want you to do.'

She thought back to last night's painful conversation with Seth. He'd been quiet when she'd told him she couldn't have children but, instead of letting him digest the news, she'd jumped to the conclusion he wouldn't want to be with her. The same way she'd assumed her father would prefer to have her as some kind of waving automaton rather than a contributing member of society without ever talking it over. She hadn't let Seth answer or discussed any option other than splitting up. She really was her own worst enemy. It was Seth who made her happy and she was only punishing herself by pushing him away.

'I've been so stupid. I told Seth we didn't need him here any more.'

'I know; he told me when he visited with Amy.'

'When?' An overwhelming sense of dread crept through her. The house had been awfully quiet this morning and Seth would never have brought Amy to work with him.

'On his way to the airport. He said there was no point in him staying any longer when I was doing so well and I'm in the hands of the best team. I don't think he wanted to disrupt his daughter's life any more than was necessary.'

Kaja barely heard what he was saying beyond that first revelation. 'He's gone?'

She might have said the words prompting that departure, told everyone including herself it was for the best, but being faced with the possibility that she would never see him again was too much. To her horror she burst into a flood of tears. That careful composure that had weathered all storms until recently slipped again. She wasn't wearing her heart on her sleeve, it was tripping down her face and splashing onto the floor.

'I thought that was what you wanted?' Her father arched an eyebrow at her, questioning her tears but with a hint that he knew the answer already.

'No. I want him to stay.'

'I could see it in his eyes that's what he wanted as well. If you're quick you might be able to catch him at the airport. If that's what you want?'

That was the million-dollar question. This was her decision and if she made the wrong choice she couldn't blame anyone else this time. She'd have to live with the consequences of what she did next for the rest of her life.

'Thanks for being our chauffeur, Fatima.' Seth hugged her before opening the boot of the car to retrieve the bags. He hadn't wanted the hassle of getting the limo and he had a hunch Fatima's offer to take them in her jalopy was so she could spend as much time as possible with Amy before they left.

'It was my pleasure. I wish you were staying.' Tears welled in her eyes and he prayed she wouldn't start crying in earnest or she'd set Amy off, and him. Neither of them really wanted to leave but Kaja wanted him gone and there wasn't anything he could do to change her mind.

He shouldn't have to. If she felt the same way about him as he did about her she would never have said the things she did. He wasn't going to hang around and prolong the agony. Leaving this way, without any fuss or dramatic showdown, left him a smidgen of dignity. He was even beginning to see why she'd walked out on him without a word five years ago. It wasn't payback, he just didn't think he could face her without giving her a good shake or breaking down in front of her.

'We have to get home.' He went to open the car door to help Amy out but Fatima grabbed his arm.

'Miss Kaja has always been afraid to do what's in her heart in case it's the wrong thing.

As a little girl she had a lot of pressure put upon her. Don't give up on her.'

'She's a grown woman now and for my sake, and Amy's, I can't do this any more. How did you know about us anyway?' They thought they'd been so careful not to let anyone know they'd ever been romantically involved, never mind that they'd rekindled their affair. It was part of the reason he was leaving so soon after being rejected. If he stayed it would become obvious to everyone how much his heart was breaking at not being able to be with her.

Fatima shrugged. 'I have known her for a very long time. She can tell me so much without saying a word. I saw the same look on her face when she came back from England as I did last night before she went to bed. I may be old but I'm not stupid, or blind. If you didn't love each other it wouldn't hurt you both so much.'

'There's nothing I can do about it now. We've made our minds up.' He opened the door and unstrapped Amy from the car seat, knowing they wouldn't carry on this conversation with her around. Fatima could call him a coward if she wished but he had more than just himself to protect this time around.

'Can't we stay a little longer, Daddy? Please?' Amy's quivering lip and big, pleading brown eyes almost made him agree to anything rather than hurt her, but he knew she'd be fine once they got home and she was back in her old routine.

'You can phone Fatima any time you want to hear her voice.'

Fatima nodded through her watery smile.

'You have my number and you're welcome to visit us in Cambridge any time.' It was unlikely this loyal mother figure would ever desert her post at the palace but he thought he should at least offer, as she and Amy had grown so close. In other circumstances he would've cultivated that bond, when they seemed to draw so much comfort from each other's company, but as things stood it was impossible.

'I won't come in with you. I'll say my goodbyes here.' She leaned down and hugged Amy as though she never wanted to let go. When she finally did, Seth saw her wipe away the tears before Amy noticed. 'Now, you be a good girl for your papa and I'll talk to you soon.'

'Thank you for everything, Fatima.' He kissed her on both cheeks, then led Amy towards the airport building, dragging their suitcase, and his heart, behind them.

'Stop the car!' Kaja's heart was hammering as she grabbed for the door handle. She'd recognised Fatima's car on the road from the airport and put two and two together. That was why the house had been unusually quiet when she'd got up. Even Fatima had gone AWOL. It was clear whose side she was taking if she'd personally driven Seth and Amy away without telling Kaja.

Fatima pulled over and wound down her window. 'I did my best to get him to stay.'

Her face crumpled and Kaja could feel her pain as acutely as her own at the loss. What had she done?

'Is it too late?' Her voice was a mere whisper, caught in her throat at the thought that she'd lost Seth and Amy for ever.

'I left them at the airport. I couldn't bear to go in and watch them fly away.'

'There might still be time. They still have to check in and go through security.' She was clutching at straws but without hope she might as well lie down on this road and weep. The talk with her father had made her realise it was up to her to take action and fight for what she wanted in life. That was Seth and Amy. She was the only one who could get them to stay and even that wasn't guaranteed.

'I tried telling him it was fear which had made you reject him. I think we both know you still love him.'

'Apparently everybody—except us—does,' she said as she got back into the limo intent on giving chase. All she needed was for Seth to believe it and be willing to give her a third chance.

They drove to the airport, lights flashing, horn blaring at any traffic so they'd let them pass. She made as many phone calls and asked for as many favours as she could en route in order to slow Seth's departure. It might make for a frustrating wait on his part but it would buy time for her to get there.

Security met her at the airport entrance after she'd called ahead and asked for their help to jump any queues. She'd purchased a flight ticket online in case she had to get on that flight to convince him she loved him. At this moment she was prepared to do whatever it took to win him back.

'Excuse us.'

'Make way, please.'

The human cordon around her moved as many travellers out of her path as they could. Kaja didn't usually take advantage of her position for her own benefit but on this occasion she was willing to use all available resources to get her man. When she got to the departure gate and saw it was empty save for the attendants at the desk, a cold sweat broke out over her skin. If she was too late she might never see him again.

'Do you have your boarding pass? The plane's sitting on the tarmac. You might just make it if you're quick.'

One last ember of hope burned a little brighter. It only took the woman a moment to scan her ticket but it might as well have been days when every second was so crucial. There was no time for niceties and Kaja snatched the boarding pass back once she was finished with it. Security hovered, uncertain of the protocol.

'I can take it from here,' she told them, then started running.

She didn't care if anyone caught a picture of her racing across the runway like a lunatic; Seth was more important than anything. It was the thought of him flying back to England and the life she'd have to endure without him that kept her legs pumping even when her lungs were fit to burst. They'd been happy together. Not just for that brief time when they'd shut out the rest of the world, but for years living together when she hadn't worried about anything except being in the moment. She wasn't going to let that simply go to waste when they might have a chance of being happy. Together.

'Wait!' she shouted at the member of the cabin crew who was getting ready to shut the door.

In her years of attending photo ops, ceremonial openings and giving public speeches she didn't remember having so many faces staring at her as she did once she stumbled on board. The whispering and gasps started off as a low rumbling, but by the time she'd made it half-way down the plane it was building up to a roar. People were turning their heads and leaning over the backs of their seats to get a better view.

'Kaja!' It was Amy who grabbed her attention first, standing up on her seat to wave while Seth gawped at her, mouth hanging open.

She rushed to his seat and knelt in the aisle. 'Seth, I'm so sorry about what I said. I didn't mean any of it.'

'Kaja, what on earth are you doing? Everyone can see you. This is going to be all over the news by the end of the day.' He was looking at all the heads peering around to see what she was doing, camera phones at the ready, not taking in what she was saying.

'I don't care. I want you to stay. I love you and I want to be with you.' It was on record now. For ever. She just didn't know if it was enough to counter all the mistakes she'd made along the way.

'You love me?' He frowned and leaned in closer for some degree of privacy. 'Only last night you told me to go. You keep blowing hot and cold, Kaja, and I'm sorry but I need stability for Amy. For my heart.'

'I'll move to England with you if that's what it takes to prove to you that I'm serious.'

'You did that once before. It didn't work out too well, remember?'

'This is different. I'm different. I thought

you'd be better off with someone who could give you the family you want and I'm sorry that I can't. All I can offer you is me.' She grabbed him with both hands and kissed him full on the lips to a plane full of whoops and cheers. This was her way of showing him she meant every word and he was all that mattered. When he kissed her back and the cheers faded into the background she knew she'd finally made the right decision.

At least Seth remembered where they were before things got too heated. 'How on earth did you manage to get here on time? I thought you were at the hospital.'

'I was. I went to see my father about going back to work and I realised I've been the one holding myself back from being happy. No more. You and Amy are my happy place. In case you didn't hear it the first time, I love you. Nothing else matters to me.'

'Then we'd better get off this plane because all I need is you. I love you too. I always have and I don't care where we live as long as we're together. Besides, I've never seen Amy so happy as I have out here. It already feels like home.' Seth took Amy by the hand and followed Kaja back down the aisle. She held her head high as the cheers rang out from the other passengers, uncaring about what they thought. All that mattered was that she was being honest with Seth and true to herself. It was all that was needed to make her happy.

This princess had never needed a prince to save her. She simply had to do it herself.

EPILOGUE

One year later

'WELL? WHAT DOES it say?' Seth was waiting for her the second she came out of the bathroom.

'We have to wait a couple of minutes.' Kaja understood his urgency when she'd been wishing away the time all through her shift in the emergency department to get to this moment. She loved her job almost as much as her husband and her stepdaughter of six months, but the anticipation had been killing her.

She'd kept the test until she got home so they could see the result together. Although that hadn't stopped Seth texting and phoning her all day once she'd told him her period was late.

Do you feel pregnant?

When do you think it happened?

Can't you take a quick break and come home?

She hoped they weren't getting their hopes up for something that might not ever happen. It seemed too good to be true after all those years she'd failed to get pregnant. Perhaps her baby had been waiting for Seth too.

'Is it time now?' Seth leaned over her shoulder, watching the window on the pregnancy test with rapt attention.

'You're worse than Fatima,' she said with a laugh. Although Fatima hadn't said anything to Kaja directly, according to Amy she'd taken to knitting lots of dolly clothes recently, 'And she doesn't even have a dolly, Kaja!' Perhaps there was something to her claims of having 'the gift' after all if she'd known something before Mother Nature.

Seth was beaming now as much as he had on their wedding day at the palace. One good thing about having such a huge family estate was they'd been able to get married in private. The ceremony had been held in the gardens with only family and friends from the hospital where they both worked in attendance. They'd only made the announcement public after their honeymoon in England, where she and Seth had been able to reminisce about the old days and tie up loose ends before he and Amy moved over for good.

'Sorry. I'm just excited.'

'I know. Neither of us thought it was going to happen.' She'd been honest with Seth that another child might not be a possibility but he'd been insistent that he still wanted a future with her. Now it seemed those impossible dreams might be about to come true.

PREGNANT

The word filling the tiny LED screen made them both gasp and stare at each other like loons.

'It's true? We're going to have a baby?' He was practically vibrating with excitement as he grabbed her into a hug.

'Yes. I'm pregnant. You're going to be a daddy again and Amy's going to be a big sister.' It was the icing on her perfect year after marrying Seth and becoming stepmother to Amy.

'You're amazing.' He held her tight and the feel of his strong arms around her was reassuring at a time where she was a little out of her depth.

'I didn't do it all on my own, you know.' The passion for one another hadn't ebbed since they'd married or moved into their own place away from the palace. Especially now they had some privacy. After the initial furore when they'd got together, the press had lost interest in a busy working mum. A happily married medic wasn't very glamorous but it was exactly the life she wanted.

'I'm going to have to book in with a midwife and organise antenatal classes. Then there's all the things we're going to need for the nursery.' A to-do list getting longer by the second popped into her head as the reality of the situation began to sink in.

'Hey. We're in this together, Mrs Davenport. I can handle all of that. I don't want you worrying about anything.' He tilted her chin up with his finger and the sheer love she saw reflected in his eyes, felt in every pore in her body, was everything she'd ever needed. Their marriage was a shared partnership and, good or bad, they would go through everything together.

'Love you, Mr Davenport.'

'And I love you. You'll always be my princess.' He kissed her on the lips, sealing the promise, and she knew when the baby came they'd be the happiest little family in Belle Crepuscolo.

* * * * *